Who ever said being poor made one a loser?
"Blessed are the poor. . . ."

Kylie shook the thought away. She would never—could never—consider living a life of poverty.

The waitress stopped at their table. "What can I get you all?" She pulled a pen from behind her ear then dropped it. Ryan reached over, picked it up, and handed it to her. "Thanks."

"You're welcome." Ryan folded his menu and then looked at Kylie. A sweet smile warmed his face, and Kylie's resolve melted. Her palms began to sweat and her heart beat faster.

"Are you ready, miss?"

Kylie looked at the waitress, determined not to think of the adorable scattering of freckles she'd noticed beneath Ryan's eyes. "Yes." She cleared her throat and clasped her hands to keep them from shaking. "I'll have maghetti and speatballs."

That's it. No more outings with the redhead.

JENNIFER JOHNSON and her unbelievably supportive husband, Albert, are happily married and raising Brooke, Hayley, and Allie, the three cutest young ladies on the planet. Besides being a middle school teacher, Jennifer loves to read, write, and chauffeur her girls. She is a member of American Christian Fiction Writers. Blessed beyond measure, Jennifer hopes to always think like a child—bigger than imaginable and with complete faith. Send her a note at jenwrites4god@bellsouth.net.

Books by Jennifer Johnson

HEARTSONG PRESENTS
HP725—By His Hand

Picket Fence Pursuit

Jennifer Johnson

Heartsong Presents

To my oldest daughter, Brooke. What a treasure you are! I'm so proud of your desire to live your life for the Lord. May you never cease to pursue Him.

Thank you, Rose McCauley, for your continual faithfulness in critiquing my work and for being such a sweet friend.

Thank you, Albert, Brooke, Hayley, and Allie, for your constant support for and patience with your loony wife and mommy.

Robin, you are such a dear friend. I thank God for you.

Lastly, praise You, Jesus, because You guide every breath I take and because You take broken vessels and make them whole. May I never stop yearning for You!

A note from the Author:
I love to hear from my readers! You may correspond with me by writing:

Jennifer Johnson
Author Relations
PO Box 721
Uhrichsville, OH 44683

ISBN 978-1-59789-429-6

PICKET FENCE PURSUIT

Scripture taken from the HOLY BIBLE, NEW INTERNATIONAL VERSION®. NIV®. Copyright © 1973, 1978, 1984 by International Bible Society. Used by permission of Zondervan Publishing House. All rights reserved.

All of the characters and events in this book are fictitious. Any resemblance to actual persons, living or dead, or to actual events is purely coincidental.

Our mission is to publish and distribute inspirational products offering exceptional value and biblical encouragement to the masses.

PRINTED IN THE U.S.A.

one

"This is what I want out of life." Kylie Andrews lifted the handle of the ice-cream machine and twirled the cone beneath the flow of the creamy, chocolate treat.

"What's that?" Robin handed Kylie a napkin.

Wrapping the napkin around the bottom of the cone, Kylie turned and handed it to the small, black-haired boy in front of the counter. He licked his lips in animated anticipation.

Kylie smiled at the urchin, then winked at her friend. "A little guy like this." Turning back to the boy, she said, "That'll be two dollars."

He pushed the money across the countertop, then shoved the tip of the ice cream between his lips. Kylie covered her mouth to avoid a giggle as the boy's eyes grew big as saucers and he shook his head. Brain freeze, no doubt. He closed his eyes and mouthed a slobbery thank-you, then turned and ran toward a man and a woman who held a baby girl.

"Kylie." Robin playfully shoved her. "You're not married. You don't even have a boyfriend."

"Yeah, but look at them. They're the perfect little family. Beautiful parents. Adorable kids. Little vacation."

Robin propped her elbows onto the counter and rested her chin in her hands. "He is a cute little guy, huh?"

Kylie looked at her longtime friend and burst into laughter. "I thought for sure he was going to pass out after taking that huge bite. I bet his head still hurts."

Robin chuckled. "Bet you're right."

Kylie swiped a wet towel out of the compact, aluminum sink and wiped her hands. "This job is a lot of fun. I'm glad you thought of it."

"Holiday World was always my favorite vacation spot as a kid. I figured if we're going to live near Santa Claus, Indiana, we might as well spend the summer working somewhere fun."

"It was really nice of your uncle to let us live in one of his apartments free of charge."

"Not exactly free. We still have to mow and keep the flowers alive."

Kylie laughed. "I'll gladly do the yard work. I've lived in a University of Evansville dorm room long enough. Mowing will be bliss."

"What about the drive?"

"The one-hour commute will be cake. We can share gas and enjoy each other's company. Even with gas prices as high as they are, a free apartment and lengthy drive is cheaper than a dorm room."

Robin nodded. "True."

"And this job is perfect—simple and stress free. One more semester of college for me, a few more for you, and we're done. *Fini*. Then it's *sayonara*, baby!"

"Yep." Robin looked at her watch. "We get off in half an hour. What do ya want to do?"

Kylie shrugged. Her happy-go-lucky mood plummeted, and she sighed. "Check my e-mail for sure."

"You gotta let that drop. You know Professor Nickels is going to give you an A. You earned it. He'll review your grades. Everything'll be fine."

"What if he doesn't?" Kylie cringed. Besides her desire to graduate with highest honors, she had to have a 3.5 grade point average to keep her academic scholarship. She'd gotten a B in Biology and couldn't afford a B in Accounting. Accounting, for crying out loud. Accounting was her major. Kylie never dreamed that Professor Nickels would be so difficult. Anyone else would have given her an A. But not Nickels the knucklehead.

"Robin, if I lose my scholarship—"

"Then you'll get a loan. Besides, you're not going to lose your scholarship."

Kylie turned away from her friend. She didn't want any more loans. She needed to be as debt free as possible when she started a job so she could help her parents.

Robin nudged her shoulder. "Let's just have fun, okay?"

"You're right." Kylie turned toward her friend just as a spoonful of ice cream launched from a pink plastic stick. She gasped when the cold, sticky goop smacked her mouth, cheek, and strands of loose hair.

"Oh, yeah." Robin danced back and forth. "I gotcha good."

"You think so, Ms. Reed?" Kylie grasped the ice-cream machine's handle, lifted, and poured a golf-ball-sized glob into her hand. She glanced at Robin, who was filling a cup from the second machine. Before Robin could finish, Kylie smacked the frozen treat onto the back of Robin's head and swooshed it around.

"You're such a good friend." Kylie rubbed her hands together and grabbed Robin in a bear hug, wiping the goop all over her friend's back. "I love you so much, Robin."

"Oh, yeah?" Robin dumped the cup over Kylie's head. "Mmm. What's that new perfume you're wearing? Chocolate drops?"

"Am I interrupting something?"

Kylie jumped at the masculine voice. Her heart beat faster and heat rushed up her neck and to her cheeks when she turned toward the man wearing a pale blue uniform that looked very much like the one she wore. A stream of cold, melting ice cream streaked down her cheek and pooled above her collarbone. She glanced at Robin, who looked as petrified as she. "I'm sorry. It won't happen again."

Wishing to crawl under the counter, Kylie grabbed several napkins from the container and wiped her cheek, neck, and hair. *Yuck. Disgusting.* She imagined the brown shade sticking to her blond hair in straight, sticky spikes around her head. She glanced at Robin, whose coal black curls were sticking straight up on the left side.

"You're not bothering me."

Kylie looked back at the man. A slow smile spread across his face, and he lifted his hands in surrender. "I just didn't want to get caught in the crossfire. My shift is about to start."

"You sure?" Robin giggled as she lifted the handle and poured a new stream into her cup. "This shade of brown would complement your red hair quite nicely."

Kylie gaped at her friend. "Robin, hush." Through gritted teeth she added, "This could get us into a lot of trouble. Ix-nay the lay-pay."

"Yeah, nix the play." He pointed at Robin, then interlocked arms with Kylie. Leaning toward her, he whispered, "I think I'll stick close to you. You must be the levelheaded one." He looked at her and cocked his head. "Actually, your hair is anything but level."

Kylie pulled her arm from his and grabbed her purse from the cabinet beside the ice-cream machines. No doubt she was a fright. Robin looked atrocious with sticky hair and chocolate handprints all over her back. "Let's go, Robin. We need to get cleaned up."

Without another glance at their relief, Kylie grabbed Robin's hand and guided her out of the cramped ice-cream concession.

"Bye. Hey, what's your. . ."

Kylie held tight to Robin's arm as she picked up the pace away from the entirely-too-cute guy and headed toward the parking lot. They had to get out of there before anyone else saw them.

"Weren't *you* in a hurry?" Robin huffed as she slid into the passenger seat, then fastened her seat belt.

Kylie stuck her key in the ignition, turned, and willed her aged Ford to start. It growled in protest, but finally it complied, and Kylie pulled out of the parking lot.

Robin popped a piece of gum into her mouth. "That guy was kind of cute. You know, in a curly-haired, hippie-looking, Richie Cunningham kind of way."

"You would think that."

"What's that supposed to mean?"

"Robin, you have to pay attention."

"Attention to what?"

"You and I both come from poor backgrounds. We want more for our children, right?"

Robin scrunched up her nose. "What's that got to do with ice-cream man?"

"Didn't you notice that he's not some young college boy? He looked like a man—older than eighteen, like closer to thirty. And, he's working at Holiday World?" Kylie looked at Robin, lifted her eyebrows, and shook her head for effect. "In my book that spells L–O–S–E–R. We can't marry losers."

"Did I ask you to marry him? I don't even remember mentioning dating him." Robin touched Kylie's shoulder. "Look, girl, you've got to get over this I-gotta-have-everything-my-way-or-no-way-and-my-way-is-perfect complex."

"What?"

"You heard me."

"So I'm a snob? Look, Robin, if I remember right, you've got to have money to be a snob."

"No you don't."

Kylie huffed. Stopping at a red light, she tapped the steering wheel and stared at a brand-new Explorer that pulled up beside her. Two girls sat in the backseat. One was trying to hit the other. A woman turned in the driver's seat and leaned around the DVD player suspended from the ceiling to scold them.

Kylie took a deep breath and exhaled. "You think I'm a snob?"

"At the moment, yes."

"Marriage is a big step. Living on love is rough." She should know. With seven siblings and a father whose income came from the coal mines, she knew all about living rough. *Even if we did have a lot of love in our home.*

Robin tapped Kylie's head. "Earth to Kylie. I didn't hear any proposals back there in ice-cream land. In fact, we don't even know his name."

"You're right. I do get crazy sometimes." Kylie sighed. *Judging. I always prejudge people. Forgive me, Lord.*

"He was cute, though."

Kylie pushed the accelerator as the light turned green. "Yeah."

"Gorgeous blue eyes. Looked like the ocean."

"Those light reddish curls were awfully cute, too."

"I totally agree."

Kylie smiled as she turned into their apartment parking space. "He wasn't too tall, but definitely not short. Not too thin, not too heavy."

"I'd say, *Goldilocks*, he was just right." Robin hopped out of the car then poked her head back in. "Race you to the door."

Kylie shook her head. "You're nuts."

"Fine, but I get the shower first."

"Wait!" But it was too late. Robin had already made it to the door and run inside.

"Great, now I get to wait, sticky and sweaty, while Robin takes her notorious forty-five-minute shower. I won't have any hot water." Kylie got out of the car and shut the door. She pried a strand of hair away from her cheek and chuckled. "Robin hit the nail on the head. He was just right."

❧

Ryan Watkins walked through the bank doors and pushed the raincoat's hood from his head. Drops of water splattered the wall and floor. Slipping out of the coat, Ryan hung it on the rack beside half a dozen other wet garments. He walked toward the teller. "Good afternoon, Mr. Richards."

His friend Michael Richards smiled. "Hey, Ryan. Gramps didn't come with you?"

"Not in this weather." Ryan opened the candy jar on the counter and scooped up three peppermints. "But I promised him a few of your goodies."

"Take as many as you'd like." Michael turned to his computer and punched several numbers. "You want your interest transferred to your checking account?"

"Yes."

"Do you want another CD like the one before?"

"Yes."

"Good. I have it ready."

Ryan grinned. "Well, Michael, aren't you on top of things?"

"I try. So, how did your grandfather's appointment go?"

"His blood pressure is still up. They had to switch his medication." Ryan grabbed the papers and pen. He was praying the new medicine worked. Gramps had already lived through one heart attack. Ryan didn't want to see him go through another. *God, You're in control.* He signed the documents, then pushed them back toward Michael. "Are you coming to the game Thursday?"

"Wouldn't miss it. Church softball is my only recreation right now."

Ryan laughed. "Are you hinting that your sweet little baby girl is keeping you up at night?"

Michael furrowed his eyebrows and shook his head. "That kid has more air in her lungs than Candy after a day of being cooped up in the house."

"Ouch. You better not let your wife hear you say that."

"Don't worry. I still love her. Both hers." Michael grinned and took the papers from Ryan. Separating the pages, Michael handed Ryan's copies to him. "I'd say our missions trip meetings will start up pretty soon."

"Yep. I'm heading to Hope to pick up some stuff today."

"I'm not sure if Candy and I will both be able to go this time. We may have to take turns until Suzanna's a little older."

Ryan nodded. "It would be hard to make a trip with a baby, especially a missions trip."

"True, but we want to take Suzanna to her birth country every chance we get. We want to be up front about her adoption."

"I'm sure you and Candy will have that girl back in Belize several times in her growing-up years."

The phone rang. Michael reached for it. "I'll see you Thursday."

"See ya then."

Ryan grabbed his raincoat and put it on. He glanced at the receipt Michael had paper-clipped to the top of the papers. His next stop was Hope Community Church to pick up several boxes of clothes, toys, shoes, eyeglasses, and other items. It wouldn't be long before he'd be on his third missions trip to Belize.

His heart sped up at the thought of wearing the clown suit and making balloon animals for the children he'd visit who had almost nothing. Remembering young Alberta's prayer of salvation on his last trip brought a smile to his face. He couldn't wait to go back.

The afternoon sped by as Ryan collected almost more than his truck could hold. He deposited the donated items at the missions team leader's house, then stopped off at a fast-food restaurant to swallow some food before work.

Having changed quickly in the staff locker room, little beads of sweat gathered on his forehead as he strode toward the small ice-cream concession. Not much larger than a child's playhouse, the place was just big enough to hold two ice-cream machines and a worker or two.

"It's like this. I'm not interested in any yahoos."

Ryan stopped at the woman's words. That sounded just like the lady from yesterday who'd been covered in chocolate ice cream. He sneaked a peek around the corner. It was her; and the same dark-haired girl was with her.

"I don't want a yahoo, either, but you're too picky," the black-haired woman answered.

"Robin, you have to have priorities."

"And I don't?"

The blond smirked, then smiled. "Did I say that?"

"All right, Ms. Hoity-Toity, what are your priorities?"

"First," she said and lifted her finger, "he must be a Christian." Ryan smiled. He agreed with her first.

"Duh," responded the one the blond called Robin.

"Second, he must love me and want a family, but not too big and not too small."

"Here we go again, Goldilocks."

The blond stomped her foot. "Do you want to hear my priorities or not?"

"Go ahead."

"He has to be strong but gentle, kind but firm, athletic but homey—"

"Homey?"

"You know, not be afraid to do the dishes, clean the toilets, and all that stuff."

"I *totally* agree with you there."

Ryan held a chuckle inside. This conversation was classic. What does a woman want? Ryan Watkins was getting the privilege of learning firsthand.

"Of course he has to have a good, stable job. Secure. I will not even consider a yahoo. Looks mean nothing."

Robin frowned. "Nothing?"

"Well, maybe a little bit. I don't want ugly kids, but gorgeous, blue eyes are at the bottom of the list."

"Let me get this straight. You want a successful, Christian husband, your own great job, and 2.5 kids. Do you also want the dog and white picket fence?"

The blond leaned against the counter. "The dog is open for discussion, but the picket fence is crucial, and yes, it must be white."

Robin flung back her head and laughed. "Why is that?"

"What perfect, established, successful family do you know that doesn't have a white picket fence?"

"You need serious help."

Red scoured up the blond's neck and flushed her cheeks. Ryan decided he'd better announce himself or the black-haired gal may end up covered in ice cream. . .again. Opening the concession door, Ryan stepped in and bowed. "One certified yahoo reporting for duty."

two

Kylie watched in horror as Robin jumped toward the stranger from the day before, wrapped him in a bear hug, and said, "Hey, Richie, what's up?"

The man chuckled. "Richie, huh? That's original. I've never heard that before."

Robin cocked her head. "Really? But you look so much like a young, long-haired Ron Howard."

"I think he's being facetious," Kylie spat behind clenched teeth. She hated when her friend acted ridiculous in front of people they didn't know. It would be one thing for her to do it alone, but Robin always chose to do it when she was with Kylie. "Robin, I think our shift is over. We need to get going. No scenes."

"Name's Ryan Watkins." The man thrust his hand toward Kylie's friend. "You must be Robin."

She giggled and grabbed his hand. "Yep, Robin Reed." Pointing toward Kylie, she added, "This here's my friend Kylie Andrews." She leaned toward him. "She's a bit on the grumpy side."

Kylie scowled at her, but Ryan threw back his head and laughed. "I think you're right. Maybe she needs a hug, too."

"Don't even think about it, you. . .you. . .curly-headed mops." Ryan frowned and looked at Robin. "Did she just insult us?"

"I think she did."

"Your curls are lovely."

"So are yours." Robin twirled a strand of hair around her finger. "You and I must go to the same barber. I believe we have the same haircut."

Ryan gasped. "I believe you may be right. I mean, aside from the fact that yours is a bit longer."

"Oh, but your curls lie so perfectly. Maybe we should make an appointment to go together."

"That's it. I've had enough." Kylie grabbed her purse from the drawer. Robin knew she hated to be embarrassed, but her *friend* was determined to make a fool of her with a complete stranger. "Find your own way home. Maybe your Bobbsey twin will give you a ride."

"Wait! That was really jerky of me, and you don't even know me." Ryan grabbed her arm. "I was just teasing. I'm a notorious teaser. I'm sorry."

"Me, too." Robin looked at the floor like a scolded puppy. "You know I'm uncontrollably silly sometimes. I wasn't trying to be mean."

Swallowing hard, Kylie forced a grin. "Of course you were teasing. I know that. I love a good joke." She choked up a laugh.

Ryan extended his hand. "Forgive me?"

"Of course." Without looking at him, Kylie accepted his hand for an instant, then grabbed her purse tighter. "Robin, are you ready to go?" She tried to sound light, but she knew this Ryan Watkins had seen to her soul. He knew he'd bruised her ego, and he was genuinely sorry.

How she wished to be more like Robin—free and glib. Instead, Kylie was sensitive and sentimental and entirely too vulnerable. She didn't like that Ryan had seen that in her.

Walking toward the car, Kylie fought to keep her chin up. She focused on trying to find her keys in her purse.

"I'm sorry, Kylie. Usually you go right along with the teasing. You know I'd never intentionally hurt your feelings. You're my best friend."

"I know. I don't know why I'm being so sensitive."

"You must like him."

Kylie gasped and gawked at her friend. "What? I—I don't even know him."

"Either that or you're worried about your accounting grade."

"The latter, I'm sure."

Kylie found her keys and gripped them in her hand. The truth was, she had gotten more upset than normal. Usually when Robin teased, Kylie laughed it off. Today, it hurt. Maybe it was Ryan's teasing that hurt.

≈

Ryan sat in the church pew, pulling miserably at his shirt collar. A dress shirt and sport coat were not his favorite attire. He'd wear them only to Sunday morning church services. And only for Gramps. Many of the congregation opted for a more casual attire, but Gramps was from the old school. A person dressed up on Sundays, and until Gramps decided otherwise, Ryan would respect that and dress up, as well.

Ryan pulled at the shoulder of his sport coat. The thing was too small. He needed to buy a new one. He sighed. *For Gramps, dressing up is a small price to pay.* At least most times it was. Today, Ryan felt as if he were suffocating.

"Why, Ryan, imagine seeing you here."

Ryan looked toward the voice that sounded very much like Robin Reed's. His mouth fell open when he saw her. "Hi." He stood and shook her hand. "I didn't know you came to church here."

"Actually, we're visiting. We attended church in Evansville for the last three years, but now that we're living near Santa Claus, we're looking for something closer. We never joined the church near school. We're hoping to find a home church now that we're getting closer to graduating."

"So you're both from Evansville?"

"Otwell, actually. Our fathers are coal miners. We've been best friends since birth, so we decided to go to college in Evansville together, too."

"How did you end up here?"

"My uncle owns an apartment building. He's letting us live in one of the apartments in exchange for keeping up the yard work." Robin smacked her hands together. "The deal was too good for two college gals to pass up."

Ryan nodded. "That's for sure. Where is Kylie?" He still felt bad for the way he'd teased her at work. Though a kidder at heart, he wasn't usually cruel. Something about her drew him, and he hadn't expected it, hadn't known how to handle it.

"Rest room."

"Oh."

"Ahem." Ryan glanced at his grandfather, who had grabbed the pew in front of him and was getting ready to stand.

Ryan grinned. "I'm sorry. Gramps, this is Robin. Robin, Gramps."

Gramps grabbed her hand and winked. "I reckon you can call me Gramps."

"I'd love to."

Kylie walked toward them. She was fumbling through her purse. "Robin, I found a couple of seats on the other side." She looked up. Her light skin flamed red. "Oh—um—I didn't see you." She looked at her bag again. "Hi, Ryan."

Ryan's heart sped up. Yes, something about Kylie definitely drew him. He could tell she had confidence, yet she seemed so vulnerable. Maybe that was what beckoned him. He'd always fought for the underdog. But Kylie wasn't an underdog. And what about the way her creamy cheeks and neck shaded crimson? He found it endearing, almost inviting.

Gramps pushed past him and grabbed Kylie's hand. "Hi, sweetie. I'm Gramps."

"Kylie." She smiled and lifted her chin. "It's wonderful to meet you."

"Won't you two sit here beside me?" Gramps pulled her hand toward him.

"Well. . ." She glanced at Ryan. He could see her confidence wane again.

"Of course we will." Robin scooted past all three of them and sat, leaving a space for Kylie to sit by Gramps.

Kylie nodded and followed Robin. Ryan inhaled cocoa butter as she passed and longed for his sunglasses, swimsuit, and a beach.

After they sat, Ryan sneaked a peek at Gramps. He patted Kylie's hand. "After the services, Ryan and I will treat you to the best Italian food you've ever tasted."

Gramps hadn't requested. He'd simply made a decision. Ryan glanced at Kylie. She smiled and nodded, but Ryan would have given a hundred bucks to cruise the inside of her mind. He had a feeling agreement wouldn't be there.

&

Kylie lifted her purse strap higher on her shoulder as she walked through the door of Marinelli's. A blast of air-conditioning blew through her hair, and she shuddered. *That's just great.* Because of her nerves, her body was already shaking of its own volition. She didn't need a second excuse.

The Sunday afternoon lunch crowd gathered around them. Ryan's grandfather and Robin moved to one side, chatting about weather conditions. Kylie knew the conversation could go on for hours since meteorology had once-upon-a-time been Robin's major and obviously the older man's favorite pastime.

Kylie moved to the other side. Something poked her in the back. She turned around to find Ryan shifting his arm around her as another couple squished through the door behind him. "Sorry."

"That's okay." Kylie shuddered again. Aggravated, she folded her arms in front of her chest. She had absolutely no reason to feel insecure, shy, or anything else in front of Ryan. He was simply a guy, a loser, in fact, according to her list of who could be considered potential date material.

She glanced at him. His light auburn curls lay softly around his head. The shaggy style appealed to her more than she'd have thought possible, in a silly, kind of goofy way.

He caught her looking at him. Heat flooded her cheeks and she averted her gaze, but not before Kylie noticed his eyes could challenge the ocean for beauty rights. She felt him looking at her. The knowledge stirred her insides, making her shudder a third time.

"Are you cold?"

"A little." She wanted to crumble under the concern in his voice.

"Here." Ryan took off his sports jacket and dropped it over her shoulders.

Why had she chosen to wear a sleeveless dress? A light sweater would have been appropriate for the middle of May. The uncommonly warm weather had her brain fuzzy. The smell of men's Obsession cologne was making it worse. She needed to sit down.

"Are you all right?" Ryan touched her arm.

She looked up at him, praying the earth would just open and swallow her whole. "I'm—"

"Watkins. Party of four."

"That's us. Take my hand."

Before she could respond, Ryan grabbed her hand and led her toward the hostess. His hand felt warm, a bit rough—and safe. Kylie focused on putting one foot in front of the other. She was determined not to think about his strong hand, his firm grip.

Once they reached the table, Ryan pulled out her chair and Kylie sat. Looking around she realized Gramps and Robin were already seated. Robin raised her eyebrows in obvious question, and Kylie looked away from her. Ryan's coat still hung from her shoulders. Kylie pondered taking it off but knew she'd shake through the whole meal. *If I act natural no one will think anything about it.*

She tried to act natural as she pushed each arm through the sleeves. Smiling, she looked around as if nothing was wrong. Her left hand knocked a glass. *Oh no.* She spied the water and tried to grab the glass. It teetered and wobbled before spilling all over the table.

Utensils clinked against the table as Ryan yanked up his cloth napkin. Robin lifted the tablecloth to keep the stream of water from landing on her, but succeeded in altering its way toward Kylie. Before Kylie could stop it, the frigid liquid poured onto her lap.

"Ah!" She jumped up, knocking her chair against the person behind her. Turning to him she shook her head, willing back tears. "I'm so sorry."

"It's okay, Kylie." Ryan stood and grabbed her arm. She faced him, and he placed a clean napkin in her hand. "It's okay."

His voice was soft and soothing, like a gentle caress. His gaze was sweet and sincere. A single tear threatened to slip down her cheek. She blinked it back as she looked at her dress. *What is wrong with me?*

Ryan gently swiped her cheek with his back of his hand. Stunned, Kylie looked up at him. Surprise washed his face, as well. He stepped back and sat in his chair.

"I'll go to the rest room with you, if you want."

Kylie stared at Robin. Realizing she still stood, she brushed her dress and shook her head. "It's just water. It'll dry."

Determined to regain control of her body and emotions, Kylie replaced her chair in its place, smiled a second apology at the man behind her, and then sat. Grabbing her menu, Kylie studied it. The words blurred, and heat rushed up her cheeks as she thought of what she must have looked like only moments before. *Stop it.* She scooted in her chair and focused harder on the menu. When the words continued to jumble, Kylie closed her eyes. *I'll just order spaghetti. Every Italian restaurant has that.*

"Do you guys know what you want?" Robin studied the menu. She opened the inside flap, then shut it again.

"My favorite is veal parmesan," answered Ryan.

"I'm getting lasagna. I always get lasagna." Gramps nodded at Ryan. "Don't I?"

"You sure do." Ryan smiled and picked up his glass of water. He took a drink. "What did you think about Pastor Chambers's sermon today?" He placed the glass back on the table.

"Good. Good. Did you see Elma's hair? The woman dyed it blue. Can you believe that? Was pink. Now, blue." Gramps snorted and shook his head.

Kylie settled back in the chair. She concentrated on keeping her breathing steady. She'd never before been such a bundle of nerves in front of a guy. Ryan wasn't even her type. He was a hippie wannabe with that shaggy haircut, or rather lack of cut. And red. She'd never liked redheads. Well, truth be told, his was a bit more of an auburn, but still it had quite a bit of red in it.

And his clothes. His red and navy blue plaid shirt was definitely a size too small and obviously uncomfortable. His khakis had seen better days, as well. Kylie had always envisioned herself with a man in a wrinkle-free, high-dollar suit that fit to exemplary perfection.

She sneaked another peek at Ryan. *And yet I'm attracted to him. Like a bee to honey. A moth to light. A magnet to metal. A poor girl to a loser.*

She sighed.

Growing up in a household of eight children with her daddy as a coal miner, Kylie knew the truth of the phrase "feast or famine." When the coal industry was going well, the Andrewses had lots of food, clothes, and fun. When the industry was down, it was free lunch at school and beans for dinner—every night.

Two of her sisters had already married coal miners. They lived the life she knew all too well. No, she wanted more. This poor girl would have nothing to do with a loser, attraction or not. God had blessed her with a good deal of intelligence and some common sense to boot. Losers were not on her list.

Who ever said being poor made one a loser? "Blessed are the poor. . . ."

Kylie shook the thought away. She would never—could never—consider living a life of poverty.

The waitress stopped at their table. "What can I get you all?" She pulled a pen from behind her ear then dropped it. Ryan reached over, picked it up, and handed it to her. "Thanks."

"You're welcome." Ryan folded his menu and then looked at Kylie. A sweet smile warmed his face, and Kylie's resolve melted. Her palms began to sweat and her heart beat faster.

"Are you ready, miss?"

Kylie looked at the waitress, determined not to think of the adorable scattering of freckles she'd noticed beneath Ryan's eyes. "Yes." She cleared her throat and clasped her hands to keep them from shaking. "I'll have maghetti and speatballs."

That's it. No more outings with the redhead.

three

The next day Ryan stood and grabbed his cell phone and wallet off his dresser and walked into the living area where Gramps had already opened the front door. His grandfather folded his arms in front of his chest. "I don't need my grandson holding my hand at the doctor's office."

Ryan blew out his breath, determined not to get aggravated with his hardheaded grandfather. "I'm going with you."

"I'm fine, I tell you." Gramps placed his newsboy cap on his head and picked up his car keys.

"Gramps, you're all the family I have left. I want to go with you."

Gramps grunted and pulled his polyester pants higher around his waist. "Fine, but I'm driving."

"Sounds like a plan."

Ryan buckled his seat belt as Gramps pulled onto the street. Gramps's bluegrass music filtered through the speakers. The older man leaned over and snapped it off. "So tell me about those girls from church."

"What about them?"

"Where'd you meet them?"

"At work."

"Mmm."

Ryan shifted in his seat. He knew his grandfather. He wanted more information than that, but Ryan didn't know what to tell him. He found himself attracted to Kylie, but he was pretty sure she was hung up on money and wanting things her way. He'd already gone down that relationship path, and he had no intentions of taking that road again.

"Tell me about the blond one." Gramps interrupted his thinking.

Ryan shrugged. "What about her?"

"A little jumpy, don't you think?"

"Yeah, she's definitely jumpy."

"A little clumsy, too."

Ryan remembered the water spilling on her dress. "Maybe, but I think she was just nervous."

"Nervous about what?"

"She was cold. I put my jacket on her shoulders—I don't know."

"If she was cold, why would wearing your jacket make her nervous?" Gramps glanced at Ryan, then back at the road. "Unless. . .she likes you a bit."

"No way. I'm a yahoo in her book."

"A what?"

Ryan shook his head. "Never mind."

Gramps pulled into the doctor's office parking lot. He took the keys from the ignition. "Well, let's get this over with."

Ryan followed his grandfather into the office. Gramps signed in and was taken back to a room within no time.

"So how are we feeling today?" A young, petite nurse took Gramps's blood pressure and pulse.

"Fit as a fiddle."

"That's good." She wrote down his numbers, then winked at him. "Dr. Hurst will be in to see you in just a moment." She opened the door and shut it behind her.

Ryan shoved his hands into his pockets. "I didn't hear her say what your blood pressure was."

"That's because she didn't."

"Don't they always tell you when they take it? Every appointment I've ever been to the nurse always tells me my weight, my temperature, my pulse, my blood pressure—"

Gramps huffed and pointed to the chair. "Would you have a

seat? You're raising my blood pressure with all your worrying."

Ryan sat and crossed his arms in front of his chest. *That man is as mule-headed as a. . .as a mule!* "I just worry about you, Gramps."

"I know, but worrying won't lower my blood pressure."

Ryan leaned back in his chair. "You're right."

The doctor opened the door, looked at Gramps's chart, and then checked him. "Well, Mr. Watkins, the new medicine seems to be doing the trick. Your blood pressure is better than mine."

Ryan sighed in relief. *Thank You, Lord.* The doctor gave Gramps his prescription and left. After Gramps buttoned his shirtsleeve, they walked to the desk, paid the bill, and headed for the car.

"Feel better?" Gramps asked.

"Much."

"I reckon I do, too."

Ryan chuckled. Gramps would never admit he'd been concerned as well. Ryan slid into the passenger's seat and buckled his seat belt.

"I'll say one thing for sure," said Gramps.

"What's that?"

"She sure is a cutie."

Ryan frowned. "The nurse?"

"No, the blond."

"What blond?"

"The gals that went to lunch with us. What was the blond's name?"

"Kylie."

"Yeah, her. Course the black-haired one was cute, too, but there was something about the blond. What do you think?"

Ryan shrugged. "She's all right."

"Just all right?"

"No. She's beautiful." Ryan looked out his window. "And

there is definitely something special about her."

❧

"Thanks for taking Robin's shift. It's probably going to be a busy day with several schools bringing their students."

Ryan smiled. "It's definitely a busy day, but I love watching all these kids. Makes me feel young."

Kylie chuckled. "Spoken like a man with experience."

"It's my fourth year working summers here."

Four years. Why would any grown man want to work here for four years? A teenager, sure. A college student, sure. She peeked at Ryan. Though he wore his hair in a younger style, Kylie felt sure he was past college age.

"I don't know if I've ever seen Robin so sick." Kylie avoided making eye contact with Ryan as she wrapped the apron around her waist.

"I hope it's nothing serious."

"Just a stomach bug, I think." She grabbed a rag and wiped off the ice-cream machine. "I was afraid you might have a daytime job that would keep you from being able to cover for her."

"Nope." He stepped in front of her, forcing her to look up at him. "This is the only place I work."

There goes that hope. She couldn't stop thinking about Ryan Watkins, from the moment she woke up to the moment she went to bed. She hoped, dreamed, prayed even, that maybe, just maybe, he had a good, solid day job and simply worked at Holiday World in the evenings because he led an otherwise boring and uneventful evening life. She turned toward the counter and began wiping it off. *Yep, one dream right out the window.*

It doesn't matter. I am the decider of my fate.

A soft voice nudged at her heart. *"I thought I was."*

She shook her head. Of course, God was the most important thing in her life. She would follow Him anywhere. She had chosen accounting as a major because He had shown her He wanted her to be there. Her life belonged to Him. She was clay in the Potter's hands.

Even in poverty?

Grabbing the broom, she squelched the thought. *I'm being silly. God wants only the best for His children. He's shown me the way, and I'm to follow it. I'm just getting a little freaked out because I'm so close to graduating—so close to finally reaching the goals He has set up for me.* "Yes, that's all that's wrong," she whispered.

"What did you say?"

She looked at Ryan. The sun seemed to glisten in his reddish hair. How could she be so attracted to Richie Cunningham, as Robin called him? "I was just mumbling to myself."

"Oh." Ryan grabbed the broom from her hand and set it against the wall. "I think you've made this place spotless." He crossed his arms and leaned against the counter. "We're going to be here awhile. Why don't you tell me a bit about yourself?"

Okay, I can do this. Small talk. No big deal. In fact, the more I learn about him, the less attractive he'll become. She smiled, grabbed a stool from beside one of the machines, and hopped onto it. "I'm an accounting major at the University of Evansville. I only have one semester left. I can hardly wait to graduate."

"That's great. What made you decide on accounting?"

"The Lord."

"The Lord?"

"Yeah, I was taking a Bible study class, asking God what my major should be. I've always loved to work with numbers. I'd kind of narrowed it down to accounting or teaching math, and I don't know how to describe it—I just felt He told me to go into accounting. Probably because I have a better chance financially with an accounting position."

"I see."

A perplexed look crossed Ryan's face, and Kylie wondered what she'd said that confused him. "Where did you go to college?"

"I didn't."

Kylie nodded. "I see." *There you have it. He already looks less attractive. One step down the "Perfect Man" ladder.*

"Hey, can we get an ice-cream cone?" A preteen girl with braces on her teeth placed her money on the counter.

"Sure can," Ryan responded before Kylie had a chance. "What can we get you?"

"I want a chocolate cone." She looked at the boy a full three inches shorter—her boyfriend, Kylie presumed. "He wants a chocolate and vanilla cone."

"You got it." Ryan smiled at Kylie. "I'll get the swirl if you'll get the chocolate."

"No problem."

They fixed the cones and handed them to the pair.

"Thanks," the youngsters said in unison and walked away. Kylie watched as the girl grabbed the boy's free hand.

"So tell me about your Lord."

"What?" Kylie looked at Ryan.

"You said the Lord led you to accounting. I was just curious about your Lord."

Kylie frowned. She'd never heard such a statement and wasn't sure what kind of response he wanted, but she'd tell him the best she could. "Well, I grew up in a large family. We attended church from as far back as I can remember. When I was eight, I felt the Lord drawing me to go forward in church. I asked Jesus into my heart and was baptized the next week." She looked up at Ryan. He seemed enthralled with every word she spoke. She swallowed as a wave of heat washed over her. "Is that what you mean?"

"Absolutely. I would have loved growing up in a big family. My parents died in a car accident when I was a teenager.

That's when I moved near Santa Claus to live with Gramps. I received Christ after that."

"Where did you live before?"

"Alaska."

"Alaska?"

"Yeah. My dad had a bit of an adventurer's heart, and when he and Mom visited Alaska for their honeymoon, he fell in love with the state. I was eleven when I had to move. I still visit sometimes."

"Do you want to live there again?"

Ryan shook his head. "Not really. Sometimes I get nostalgic about it, but Gramps is all the family I have now, and I want to be near him."

"It's good you live so close that you can take him to church."

Ryan chuckled. "First of all, the man hardly ever lets me take him anywhere. He loves to drive. Second, we live in the same house. So like it or not, and sometimes he does make me crazy, we are definitely close enough to go to church together."

He's so poor he has to live with his grandfather. Getting to know each other was the best idea Ryan Watkins ever had. She smiled up at him. His hair didn't glisten all that much, and his eyes didn't seem quite so swimming. Another step down the ladder.

"That teen over there. He's been lurking around awhile, hasn't he?" Ryan nodded to the adolescent standing beside a bench. His hair was unkempt and looked dirty. His clothes, worn and torn in places, were worse than his hair. The teen looked in his wallet, then at the ice-cream stand, then back at his wallet.

"I don't know." Memories of being sponsored for school trips washed over Kylie. She remembered friends' parents who'd generously spotted her a few dollars for lunch or snacks. They never seemed to mind, but Kylie had.

"Hey, buddy." Ryan held an ice-cream cone in one hand

and motioned with his free hand for the boy to come to the stand.

The adolescent sauntered over, his face hardened, and his hand tightly clutched his wallet. "What?"

"I've got an extra ice-cream cone here. Just wondered if you'd like to have it."

The teen's eyes lit for a moment and then clouded. "Don't need no charity. If I want an ice cream, I'll buy an ice cream."

Ryan shook his head. "Ain't charity, man. I just thought you might like an ice-cream cone."

"Everyone else has to buy one. Why not me? Sounds an awful lot like charity."

Kylie tried to swallow the knot that formed in her throat. She knew exactly how the boy felt. She hated charity. Loathed it. How could Ryan do this? The ice cream wasn't worth it to the teen. He'd rather go without than always be beholden to one person or another.

Ryan leaned against the counter. "I'm not going to lie to you, man. Everyone else does have to pay, but sometimes in life people like to give a little gift to other people. I'm not seeing you as charity. I just simply bought an ice-cream cone." Ryan grabbed money from his pocket, opened the cash register, and dropped it in. "And I want to give it to you. Now, are you going to take it or not?"

The teen seemed to search Ryan's expression. Finally, he exhaled. "Sure, I'll take it."

Kylie watched as the adolescent walked away, licking his ice-cream cone. She looked back at Ryan, who'd already turned away to wipe off the machines. Ryan's heart was as genuine as the mop of reddish hair atop his head.

That's just great. The guy falls two steps down the ladder and hops three steps up.

four

"This is going to be fun." Robin hooked arms with Kylie.

"Fun," Kylie mumbled as she picked a wisp of hair out of her lipstick-covered lips and pushed it behind her ear.

"Come on, Kylie, have a little fun. You got your grades today." She wiggled and bumped her hip against Kylie's. "Professor Nickels gave you the A."

Kylie smiled. Pure satisfaction filled her heart. "I earned that A, my friend."

"Yes, you did. Now, loosen up and let's have a little fun."

"You're on."

Kylie quickened her step, and Robin fell in line with her. The twosome pushed open the church's recreation center doors. A banner on the far wall read SINGLES' GAME DAY. Queasiness filled Kylie's stomach.

"Don't get nervous," Robin whispered in her ear and squeezed her arm for reassurance. "This will be a blast."

"You know me too well."

"Yep, and you'll be fine." Robin let go of Kylie's arm and winked at her. "Let's go sign in."

Kylie placed her name tag on her shirt and listened as a large, brown-haired man announced different groups. "In group three," the man's voice boomed over the speakers, "Kylie Andrews, Mike Dickerson, Cami Longman. . ."

Kylie listened, praying he would announce Robin Reed in her group. She clutched her purse strap.

"Sandy Osborne, Zane Sanderson. . ."

Kylie's heart plummeted. He was reading in alphabetical order. Robin wouldn't be in her group.

"You'll have fun," Robin whispered and squeezed her arm once more.

"And Ryan Watkins." The announcer stopped and pointed to a group of chairs in one corner. "Group three will meet right there."

"Hey, somebody I know," Ryan's voice sounded from behind her.

Robin laughed. "I'm glad you're here. Kylie gets so nervous. She'll already have a friend in her group."

"Robin," Kylie spat through clenched teeth. She was a great friend, but she had precious little tact.

"I'm glad to have a friend in my group, too."

Kylie looked up at her male "friend." His gaze spoke nothing but sincerity and kindness, and she willed her nerves to calm. "Let's go, then."

They walked to the group and sat beside each other on metal folding chairs. The group's leader, a tiny brunette, bounced around the circle, introducing herself to everyone. She stopped, clapped her hands, and exhaled. "I've already told you my name is Macy. We're going to have a great time today. I know we will build lifelong friendships—and who knows, maybe our perfect, God-intended match." She looked at Ryan and winked.

She did not just wink at him. Kylie peeked at Ryan, who simply grinned and leaned back in his chair. *What do I care if she winked at him?* She placed her purse under her chair, then crossed her legs. *What do I care if he grinned at her wink?*

Kylie sneaked another peek at Ryan. This time he glanced at her and winked. She forced a smile and looked away. *The nerve of him. Flirting with me after the cute little group leader flirted with him.*

"Okay, the first thing we're going to do is get to know each other," bubbled Macy. "I've copied Bible verses onto slips of paper. I'll pass them out, you'll read the verse silently, and then tell us your name and what the verse means to you in your walk with Christ."

Kylie trembled at the thought of sharing such personal information with a group of twelve strangers.

"I'm sorry. Putting the cart before the horse." Macy smacked the side of her leg and snorted at her mistake. Even her snort sounded cute. "I'm going to pair you up for this activity, then we'll go to a group game." She walked around the circle. "You and you. You and you." She pointed to Kylie and Ryan. "You and you."

Ryan turned toward Kylie. "This is great. We already kind of know each other."

"That's true." Kylie wasn't sure she was quite as thrilled to be paired with a man whose cologne made her weak in the knees and whose too-long, wavy hair attracted her in the weirdest of ways.

"You want to go first or you want me to?"

"I think I want to get it over with." Kylie read through her verse and smiled. It fit her life perfectly. She looked at Ryan. "You ready?"

"Whenever you are."

Kylie shifted in her chair. "Okay. You already know I'm Kylie. My verse is Proverbs 21:21. 'He who pursues righteousness and love finds life, prosperity and honor.'"

"That's a great verse."

"Yes, and it's perfect for me to share. I think I've told you I was raised in a large family, eight kids to be exact."

Ryan's eyes bulged. "You're kidding."

"Not kidding. We were pretty poor most of the time. My dad was a coal miner. He and Mama grew up in eastern Kentucky, and for the first few years of their marriage, Daddy worked in Pike County. By the time Mama was pregnant with me, times were pretty rough. He was offered a job in Otwell, and they've lived there ever since. Still, if you know anything about coal mining, you'd know life is feast or famine, and with ten mouths to feed, it was often famine."

"But what a blessing. You never lacked a playmate."

Kylie laughed. "That's true. I also never enjoyed some peace and quiet or the ability to have a few personal items that no one messed with, but as a kid I *wanted* both!"

"I bet it was hard to keep your siblings out of your stuff."

"Definitely. Anyway, even as a small girl I knew God wanted me to pursue more than the life I led." She uncrossed her legs and rested her elbows on her knees. "Two of my sisters have already married coal miners, and life is hard for them. Well, now I'm about to graduate from college. I plan to get a good job and marry a man with a steady income. I will pursue righteousness for the love of my family. I'll be able to help them."

Ryan's brows furrowed into a deep frown. "I don't understand how you're getting 'be rich and marry rich' from that verse."

"Don't you see—the verse says 'He who pursues righteousness and love'—I'm getting my degree to get a good job. It's a righteous pursuit for the love of my family." Kylie read the rest of her verse. " 'Finds life, prosperity and honor.' God will give me prosperity, because my pursuit is to help my family."

"So, your family resents the coal mining business?"

"Well, no."

"Then they hate the poverty that goes up and down with it?"

Kylie remembered the many times her mother had made a game out of the unusual concoctions of dinner menus, like beans and corn bread with a side order of pancakes. As kids, they'd loved to guess what their mom would conjure up. "Well, not really."

"So, is your pursuit really from God?"

How dare he challenge her walk with the Lord! Ryan Watkins hardly knew a thing about her. He had no idea what her life had been like. He obviously had family willing and ready to let him mooch off them. She was not and would never again be a charity case. God gave her a capable mind and two capable hands with which to provide work—hard work. She could hardly wait to help her family, to buy food during the down times, and to buy clothes for her siblings and nephews. "Yes, my pursuit is definitely from God."

&

"Kylie, I really like him."

"Robin, you don't even know him."

Ryan didn't mean to eavesdrop, but the two were only a few feet away from him. He twisted in his chair in an attempt not to listen.

"But I feel an instant connection," Robin responded.

"You always move too fast. You don't think things through. What do you know about him?"

"He's a Christian. A youth minister, in fact. He has a small son."

Kylie gasped, and Ryan couldn't help but pay attention now. "He has a child?"

"It's not like that. Tyler's wife died from leukemia when their son was three."

"Oh, Robin, haven't you heard of serial murderers who pick up young women at functions like these? They fill women's heads with garbage."

"Lots of people know Tyler." Robin scanned the room and then poked Ryan in the back. He cringed. Tyler was a great guy, but there was no way Ryan wanted to be in on this discussion. "Ryan, do you know Tyler Pettry?"

"Uh, yeah." Ryan took a slow drink of his pop.

"Is he a serial murderer?"

Ryan choked back his laugh. "I hope not. He leads our youth."

Robin patted Kylie's back. "There you have it. Probably not a serial murderer."

Kylie crossed her arms in front of her chest. "Fine. At least the utilities are paid this month, so if you don't come home because"—Kylie unfolded her arms and pointed to her chest—"*I told you so*, then at least I won't have to pay them by myself."

Ryan smiled at Kylie's dramatics.

Robin punched Ryan's arm and then hugged Kylie. "I'll see you tonight, girlfriend."

Ryan watched as Robin walked out of the building with Tyler. He gazed back at Kylie, whose expression was sour as a lemon drop.

"I think I'll head on home," Kylie muttered. She opened her purse and searched inside. "Oh, no."

"What is it?"

"Robin drove today, and she didn't leave me her car keys."

"I'll see if I can catch them." Ryan raced out the door as Tyler's Camry turned onto the main road. He walked back to Kylie. "They're gone."

Kylie placed her cell phone back in her purse. "Robin doesn't have her phone on." She slouched into a chair and placed her hand on her head.

"I'll take you home, Ki."

"What did you call me?"

Ryan tried to replay what he'd said. "I don't know."

"You called me Ki. I haven't heard that since before my granny died."

"I'm sorry." Ryan shoved his hands into his pockets. "I didn't mean to offend you."

"It's all right." Kylie picked at a chip in her fingernail polish. "It was kind of nice to hear it again."

Ryan grabbed her hand and helped her up from the chair. Her skin, soft beneath his, felt nice and warm. "I'll take you home."

"I'd appreciate it."

She'd softened somehow. Despite their disagreement about

the verse, despite Robin's leaving with a serial murderer/ youth minister. Ryan found himself drawn to this side of the woman.

Kylie was smart. She was beautiful with her long, silky blond hair, sprinkling of freckles beneath blue eyes, and the cutest dimple in her chin he'd ever seen. She was loyal to family and friends, and he could sense her love for the Lord, even if her understanding of scripture seemed quite misguided.

Which is exactly why I must keep up my guard. The last thing I need is another well-meaning woman like Vanessa Bailey in my life and heart.

Yes, he'd have to stay alert when it came to Kylie Andrews. Ryan had believed Vanessa to be his one and only, and she was sweet as honey until she learned of Ryan's true material worth. Ryan had no intention of lording his wealth over others. After spending his preteen years watching his dad slave away at a logging company, God gave Ryan the machine idea that made cutting logs less strenuous for the workers and still more efficient for the owners. God also allowed him to sell the blueprints to an Alaskan company. And it was God who blessed him with the revenue that could have been squandered in a year or two's time had it not been for his investing-savvy grandfather who'd put chunks of money in several good stocks and bonds and taught Ryan how to manage his assets and make them grow.

Ryan wasn't rich, but he would never want for anything, either. Because he loved giving to others, he took small jobs like at the amusement park and as a Santa at the mall in Evansville during Christmas. He didn't want others to know. The gifts, the ministry trips—they were between him and God.

"You want to grab a bite of dinner on the way?"

He watched as Kylie tensed as she seemed to contemplate the offer. "Robin and I desperately need to go to the grocery, so I think I'll take you up on that."

They began to walk toward his car. "Mind if I drive by the house and pick up Gramps?"

Kylie smiled and relaxed. "That would be great."

Ryan opened her door. As she slid into the passenger seat, Ryan caught a whiff of her hair. The floral scent was nice. He imagined running his fingers through the length of it. *Get a grip, man.* He shut the door and moved to the driver's side.

"I don't live too far away." He put the keys in the ignition and started the car. "Gramps will enjoy having someone besides me to talk to."

"You don't get along?"

Ryan laughed. "We just see a lot of each other."

He turned onto the secluded road that led to his house. Anxiety welled inside him as he drove nearer. What would Kylie think of his home? Why did it matter what she thought?

Within moments, the top of his white, colonial-style house came into sight. It wasn't overly large, but Ryan had built a good-sized home, one that would, hopefully, be filled with children someday. Full-grown trees dotted his property. Flowers and bushes, strawberry vines and blackberry bushes, even a vegetable garden spotted the front and backyard. Gramps loved to work with nature.

His wraparound porch sported a swing, wicker furniture, and rocking chairs. Gramps sat in one of the chairs, reading a science-fiction novel as he rocked back and forth.

He glanced at Kylie. An expression of pleasant awe covered her face. "This place is amazing. It's beautiful."

"Thanks." Ryan relaxed in his seat. He had no choice but to admit it. What she thought meant a whole lot.

❧

Kylie hesitantly waved at Ryan's grandfather as she stepped out of the car. The man smacked his book shut and hopped up from the rocking chair.

"Well, hello there, Kylie. It's great to see you. Wonderful

evening, don't you think?" Gramps covered the distance between them and shook her hand.

"Yes. The weather's very nice." She looked from him to Ryan. "You have a beautiful home."

Ryan's gaze fell to the ground, then back up to hers. "Thank you."

His eyes seemed to penetrate her soul, sending tingles through her body. "You're welcome."

Ryan turned toward his grandfather. "Gramps, we were heading to town for a bite to eat. Thought you might like to go."

"I just fixed up a big pot of vegetable soup. The corn bread'll be done in about ten minutes. Why don't you two just stay here and eat?"

Kylie grinned at the older man. *What a sweetie.* She'd fall flat on her face if she ever walked into her parents' house and found her daddy or one of her three brothers fixing a meal. Of course, Ryan and Gramps did live alone. "I'd love to stay."

Ryan lifted his eyebrows. His look of surprise made Kylie realize she hadn't been her true self around the man. She'd remedy that today.

"Great." Gramps grabbed her hand and led her into the house. "Ryan, take her on a tour, and I'll get the corn bread out of the oven."

For the first time embarrassment and uncertainty wrapped Ryan's features. He motioned for her to follow him into one room after the other. She loved the homey feel of the house, although it definitely had a bachelor's edge. He took her into a room upstairs. Pictures from a tropical-looking region sat on a table and hung on the walls. She leaned down and looked at a picture of a family standing in front of a small home.

"That's a family from Belize." Ryan picked up the frame and handed it to her.

"Belize?"

"Yes, it's a small country in Central America. I go there with a group on missions trips."

"Oh." Kylie studied the man before her. He gave away ice-cream cones and went on missions trips. What other secrets would she discover about the man?

"Our group fixed their home. It had been damaged by a storm."

"That's really neat. I've always wanted to go on a missions trip."

"We're having a meeting next week. We'll be going again in January."

"Really?"

"I'd love to have you go with us."

"I think I'd like to go." She peered up at Ryan, realizing there was more to him than she'd originally thought. *I'm actually looking forward to getting to know him better.*

five

Kylie watched as the missions trip video showed a doctor examining a small boy's mouth. She listened as the speaker shared about the multitude of children in Belize who received medication and vitamins from the ministry's effort.

A single tear slipped down Kylie's cheek before the picture switched to show a clown making animal balloons for a group of children. Her heart pounded within her chest when a boy jumped up and down, then smiled fully for the camera when the clown handed him a red giraffe.

Ryan leaned close and whispered in her ear, "That's me."

"That's you?" She turned toward him and studied his profile. *Who are you, Ryan Watkins? I've never met anyone like you.*

She watched wrinkles form at the corners of his eyes as his smile grew. Pleasure in serving "the least of these" surrounded his face and seemed to seep from his very pores. "Yeah. I love to see the children's faces light up when I make balloon art for them."

"I'm sure it's wonderful."

"The children have almost nothing. They get so excited over the smallest gifts."

She looked back at the video. In the film, Ryan the clown turned toward the camera, making a honking noise as he squeezed his oversize, red-ball nose. He waved as he lifted a toddling child in his arms. The child squeezed his nose, as well.

God, I want what Ryan has. I've loved and served You for as long as I can remember, but there's something different about him. Something—more.

The video ended and Kylie listened as a pastor from a sister church talked about ministry opportunities available for people who would like to join their trip to Belize. "Of course, the people need to be examined by nurses, doctors, and dentists. We need carpenters, electricians, and plumbers to help with home and church needs."

The pastor grabbed a packet filled with crayons, glue, scissors, and other items. He held it up before the group of potential short-term missionaries. "But we also hold a vacation Bible school. If you can color with a child, help a mother by holding her baby so she can teach Bible school, or even dress up like a clown—"

Ryan clenched his fists over his head and pumped his arms as if he'd just won a race. Kylie giggled and pushed him with her shoulder.

The pastor laughed. "As I was saying, you could dress up like a clown as our good friend Ryan does on every trip."

Kylie looked at Ryan. "You've gone on every trip?"

He nodded. "Every one."

The pastor continued. "Anything you can do is a huge help. Simply telling others what Christ has done for you is the greatest ministry you can give."

Kylie leaned back in her chair. She couldn't remember the last time she'd shared her faith with someone. The idea of it sent nervous but excited tingles through her body.

The pastor's voice interrupted her thoughts. "Remember in scripture when Peter and John went to the temple in Jerusalem. There was a lame beggar sitting in front of the gate called Beautiful."

Kylie crossed her legs and touched her chin in contemplation. There were several beggar stories in scripture. She wasn't sure which one he referred to.

The pastor went on. "Peter told the beggar he didn't have any silver or gold." He lifted his finger in the air. "But Peter said what he could give, he would. So he healed the man in Christ's name that very moment." The pastor spread his arms open. "Friends, God has given us different talents and abilities. What we can give, let's give."

Kylie's stomach turned and her heart raced. She wanted to go on this missions trip. She didn't have any medical or construction talents, but she could definitely hold a baby.

A middle-aged woman walked to the front of the group. "Understand, friends, funding has to be raised on an individual basis. Our ministry is not supported by any federal or state missions boards." She showed a presentation that broke down the cost of the trip.

Kylie gasped when the woman reached the final total. *Money!* Her heart plummeted. *It's always about money.*

꙳

"Well, what did you think?" Ryan started the car and pulled onto the road.

"It sounds wonderful."

Ryan could hear the hesitation in her voice. Why, he wasn't sure. He saw the lone tear slide down her cheek during the video. Her excitement was evident, magnetic even.

"But?" Ryan took in the look of frustration wrapping her features. "There's a problem, huh?"

"I don't know."

"It can't be school. You'll graduate in December."

"That's true."

He pulled into her apartment building's parking lot and turned off the car. Shifting in his seat, he looked at her. She'd pulled her long hair into a ponytail. The wind allowed several blond strands to escape around her ears and the nape of her neck. Baby hairs, he'd once heard someone call them. Her skin, so light, looked almost porcelain, like the sun had never touched it. She was a true beauty on the outside. The more time he spent with her, he saw it on the inside, too.

So, why wouldn't she want to go? The truth hit him in an instant. "Is it the money?"

"It's always the money." She didn't look at him but kept her gaze focused on the windshield.

"No prob—" Ryan stopped. He longed to tell her he'd pay her way, to tell her money was not an inkling of an issue. But he couldn't. Not yet. "I'll help you raise the money."

Kylie huffed. "What about yours? Don't you have to raise your own?"

"God always provides."

"I wish I had your faith." She grabbed her purse off the floorboard and opened the car door. "Look," she said, turning back toward him, "I really want to go. And you *are* right. If God wants me there, He will provide."

She shut the door. Ryan watched as she walked up the sidewalk. She unlocked the door, then waved back at him. "Thanks for taking me, Ryan."

She disappeared into the apartment. Ryan sat for several seconds. Kylie wasn't like any other woman he knew. Her love for the Lord was there, evident, and that quality meant more to him than anything else. She also had a wonderful personality, and she cared—truly cared—for the people in her life, like her family and Robin. And her looks? There was no question he was physically attracted to her.

But the money. He knew she'd grown up poor. Knew she had a passel of sisters and brothers. Knew life had been tough for her. She'd shared as much with him, but what was her hang-up? Many people grew up in financially difficult situations, but they didn't resent their pasts or gear their futures on account of it. Ryan growled at the steering wheel. "She stated the problem from her own lips. For some people, it's always about the money."

six

"I can't believe you landed an interview at Miller Enterprises."
Robin grabbed Kylie's arm and shook it in excitement.

Kylie laughed. "I know. It's my dream job. I didn't think I'd
have a chance for an interview like this until I'd worked ten
years or more."

"And you're not even graduated!"

"I know! I figured I'd do the books for some mom-and-pop
store for a while, get some experience, then maybe land a good
interview somewhere. But Miller takes care of all the accounting
for several major businesses in Evansville." Kylie's hand shook as
she took her lipstick from her makeup case and applied it to her
lips. "I think you need to pinch me or something."

"No, I just need to borrow your pink flip-flops." Robin raced
into the other room.

"What?"

Robin held up Kylie's hot pink, daisy-covered sandals.
"These."

"Okay, but why?"

"Tyler and I are taking Bransom on a picnic."

Kylie studied her friend's reflection in the mirror. "You've
been spending a lot of time with Tyler."

"I know." Robin combed her curls, then fluffed them back
into place.

"A lot of time."

Robin turned toward Kylie. "I'm going to honest; I like
Tyler—a lot. A lot, lot."

"You know when school starts back you won't have as much
time for—"

"I'm not even thinking about when school starts back. I haven't been as focused as you. I still have a full two years ahead of me *if* I figure out what major I want."

"What are you saying?"

"I'm not saying anything."

"It sounds to me like you're saying something."

"Kylie, I'm not thinking about school. I'm not as gung ho as you. I'm taking life one day at a time." She wrapped her arms around Kylie. "I don't want to talk about this. You go to that interview and knock their socks off."

"But, Robin—"

Robin pulled away, grabbing both of Kylie's forearms. "It's not the time for us to talk about this. You go to that interview and show them what a wonderful person you are."

Kylie let out a long breath and smiled as she squeezed her friend in a tight hug. She let go and grabbed her keys from the bathroom counter. "You're right, but we *are* going to talk later."

As she bounded through the apartment, she grabbed her briefcase off the couch and headed out the door. "God," she whispered, "You know all things. You know how much I want to help my family. This feels like my chance."

&

"Come on in," Gramps's voice sounded from the entry.

Ryan grabbed an oven mitt, opened the oven door, and lifted out the yeast rolls. Whoever had stopped for a visit was in for a treat. Ryan had grilled thick T-bone steaks and aluminum-wrapped potatoes, green peppers, and onions mixed with butter and garlic salt. Gramps had boiled corn on the cob and tossed a salad.

"Take off that little sweater you got on. We're about to have supper, and you're staying," Gramps's voice boomed through the house.

"Really, I didn't mean to impose. I didn't realize you'd eat this early."

"Kylie?" Ryan pulled the oven mitt off. *That sounded just like her. What is she doing here?*

"Girl, you're not imposing on anyone. You're going to stay right here and eat." Gramps nudged Kylie into the kitchen.

"Don't you look nice." Ryan drank in her blond hair, soft and loosely pulled up. Her cheeks flushed, making her eyes a deeper blue. Her navy suit didn't look half bad, either.

"Thanks." She cupped her hand over her mouth. "I like your apron."

Ryan glanced down at his pink polka-dotted apron with lace fringe. His face burned as he untied the strings around his waist. "It's a joke between me and Gramps."

"I have no idea what he's talking about." Gramps inhaled and shook his head. "It embarrasses me each and every time he puts that thing on."

"Gramps!"

Kylie giggled. "I think it's great. How does the saying go— 'Real men wear pink'?"

Ryan pounded his chest with his fist. "Yep, and I'm a real man." He laughed. "Okay, enough of that." He grabbed another plate from the cabinet. "Let's eat and you can tell us why you're here."

"I really didn't mean to impose."

"Do you think we can eat all this ourselves?" Ryan waved his hand across the counter.

Kylie grinned. "You are two grown men, and my brothers could do it."

Ryan lifted his eyebrows. "Probably true, but we want to share. Now eat."

He moved closer to her, shoving the plate in her hand. Her perfume lingered as she moved over to the table. Ryan relished it for just a moment longer than necessary as he fixed his own plate. Once Gramps was ready, Ryan blessed the food.

He looked up as Kylie took a sip of her pop. *I like seeing her here, Lord. This feels right.* She crinkled the napkin in her hand, and Ryan glanced up to find her blushing. *She knows what I'm thinking.* Ryan continued to stare into her eyes. He couldn't deny it. He was falling for her.

"So what brings you out here?" said Gramps.

Ryan blinked, grabbed his knife and fork, and began cutting his steak.

"I have wonderful news." Kylie placed her napkin in her lap.

"What is it?" asked Ryan.

"I had a job interview at Miller Enterprises today."

"What's Miller Enterprises?" asked Gramps.

"A large accounting firm in Evansville. They handle the books for several businesses. It's like my dream job."

"That's terrific." Ryan smiled. Her excitement was contagious.

"Mmm-hmm, and it went great, too. I've got the job. I start at the end of January."

"Congratulations." Gramps stood and shook her hand.

"Thanks, and I should be able to go on the missions trip with you." She looked at Ryan with such anticipation he thought his heart would burst.

"I'm really happy for you. It's just what you've wanted."

"Yes. Isn't God amazing?"

"He's definitely amazing."

Ryan listened as Kylie chattered about the interview, the position, and how God had given her the desires of her heart. Contentment welled in his own heart as he thought of sharing excitement and sadness, success and failure, up and down on a daily basis with her. The more she spoke, the more Ryan wanted to hear, and the more he wanted to know.

God, I'm falling hard, and I like it. He closed his eyes for a brief moment. *I'm going to trust You with my heart.*

"Let me help you with those dishes." Kylie stood and stacked the plates.

"You don't need to do that." Ryan took them from her hand.

"It's the least I can do." She gazed up at him and puckered her lip. "Please."

Everything in him wanted to draw her close and kiss her. He swallowed and turned toward the sink. "Okay, you can help."

Pretending to focus on getting the water to the right temperature, Ryan stilled his anxious thoughts.

"You're a pretty good cook." Kylie picked up the salad bowl and the dressing bottles. She had taken her hair out of its knot and let it flow down her back. Its softness called to him, and he had to look away again.

"I'll have to return the favor sometime." She walked toward him. Once again her sweet perfume sent his senses into overdrive.

"Sounds good." Ryan plunged his hands into the soapy water.

"I can't believe you don't have a dishwasher. Two bachelors doing manual dishes." Kylie winked and smiled, sending his brain into a frenzy.

"Look, Kylie." Ryan yanked his hand out of the water, sending bubbles through the air. Several hit her face. She scrunched her nose and spit them away.

"Yeah?" She wiped them away, smudging bubbles across her cheek.

She couldn't possibly look any cuter than she does right now with bubbles streaked across her face. "I'm sorry." He grabbed a paper towel and wiped her cheek. Allowing his hand to linger, he gazed into her eyes. "What I'm trying to say is, would you like to go out to dinner this Saturday?"

"As a date?"

"As a date."

Kylie blinked. "O–kay."

Ryan cupped her chin in his hand. "I can't wait."

seven

"What was I thinking?" Kylie stared at her closet. Nothing looked appealing.

"You were thinking that Richie Cunningham is quite the cutie. That you'd love to run your fingers through that long, curly mop."

"Ugh." Kylie pretended to gag. "You make his hair sound disgusting."

"You and I both know it's not disgusting. He has the most unique color and style I've ever seen." Robin wiggled her eyebrows. "And it's adorable."

Kylie grabbed a bright orange T-shirt and an aqua polo shirt with pink and white stripes from her closet. She turned toward Robin. "Which one?"

"Definitely the aqua. It brings out your eyes and complements your fair skin."

Kylie leaned against the dresser and studied her face in the mirror. "I hate my coloring."

"Don't get me started on that again. Do you know how many people would kill to have your perfect complexion? And that sprinkling of the cutest freckles across your cheeks and nose to boot? I spent my entire teenage life fighting pimples and blackheads."

"Oh no, here we go."

"Here we go is right." Robin hopped off her bed and tugged Kylie's arm. "I spent years in a dermatologist's office—"

"And my skin still doesn't look as good as yours." Kylie finished Robin's sentence and stuck out her tongue. "Fine. I won't complain about my skin color."

51

"Thank you." Robin crossed her arms in front of her chest and feigned frustration. One side of her mouth lifted in a grin. "So, where's Richie taking you?"

"Dinner, I think."

"Casual?"

"He didn't say, so I'm going with khaki capris and a nice top. I figure I can wear that to fast food or to a halfway decent restaurant."

"Sounds like a plan." Robin grabbed Kylie's arm and squeezed. "Listen, let yourself have fun. I want to hear all the juicy details tonight." She picked up her purse, then slid on her sandals.

"Where are you going?"

"Out."

"With Tyler?"

"Yep."

"Robin, you've spent a lot of time with him, like almost every waking hour for the last few weeks. You even got Ryan to cover for you at work one day."

"Yep."

"We need to talk about this. What are you going to do when school starts?"

"I told you I'm not worried about that. One day at a time."

"Robin—"

"Look, Kylie, Tyler is a wonderful Christian man. Bransom is a super kid. I love them." Robin faced Kylie. "Both of them."

Kylie sat on the edge of the bed as her stomach tied in knots. "Are you saying—"

Robin nodded. "Yes, I am." She kissed the top of Kylie's head then headed for the door. "I'll see you later."

Before Kylie had a chance to respond, Robin was gone. "Oh, my. What is she thinking?"

She stood, grabbed the aqua polo, and pulled it over her

head, then slid into her capris. After applying a touch of blush and mascara, she brushed her hair, deciding to let it fall straight and silky down her back.

She looked at her alarm clock. "I still have forty-five minutes until he gets here." While puttering around the apartment, straightening magazines and fluffing pillows, she noticed her bank statement on the coffee table. "Might as well balance my checkbook before he comes."

After scooping it off the table, she grabbed her purse from the counter and searched through it for her checkbook. "This probably isn't the best of ideas." She opened the cupboard and picked up the calculator. "This always makes me grouchy."

After sliding into a dining room chair, Kylie spread her papers on the table. It didn't take long to figure the numbers and discover she had ten dollars less than she thought in the account due to a subtraction error. "Not too bad of a mistake." She wrote her current balance in the ledger and then flipped her checkbook pages to find the calendar. "Don't have much to live on 'til payday, though."

Exhaling, she smacked the checkbook shut, collected the statement and calculator, and put them away. "I hate being broke."

Her mind wandered to Robin. What was her friend thinking? She needed to keep her head, to finish school, not to fall head over heels for the first guy she dated. Kylie didn't deny Tyler being a great guy. She didn't even have a problem with Robin falling in love with him, marrying him, and having children with him, but her friend needed to finish school first. She needed to be able to support them if something tragic happened.

Of course, Tyler won't be getting black lung from his job. Kylie closed her eyes and thought of her parents. Only four of her brothers and sisters still lived at home. Two of them worked to support the family until Daddy's disability claim could be settled. Coal mining had sucked the life from her family.

Her mind skipped to Ryan. He was a true gem, the kind of man she would want to marry, have a few kids with, a dog, and a white picket fence, but he wasn't a provider. "He's an ice-cream-cone clerk at an amusement park." She smacked her thigh. "I need a provider."

She looked at her watch again. He should arrive in fifteen minutes or less. She walked into the bathroom and brushed through her hair one last time. After pulling her lipstick from the drawer, she put some on and smacked her lips together. "Tonight, I'll tell him we can only be friends."

❧

Ryan couldn't remember the last time he'd felt this way. He was downright giddy. Truly unmasculine, that was for sure. He squelched the excitement inside him as he opened the restaurant door for Kylie. The host seated them, and Ryan picked up the menu.

"Do you know what you want?" Kylie asked before he'd had a chance to read what they offered.

He chuckled. "Not yet."

"I always get the shrimp platter."

"Good, huh?"

"Yeah."

"I'll trust your judgment and just go with that."

"Oh, I didn't mean. . ."

Ryan frowned. Kylie was nervous, and he couldn't figure out why. Maybe just because this was their first date. One of many, if he had his way. "I love shrimp. I'm sure it will be great."

He put down the menu. He watched as Kylie played with her silverware for several moments then scanned the room, looking anywhere but at him. *Small talk. . .think of something to say.* "So, how do you like working at Holiday World?"

"It's good."

"Great." Ryan fiddled with the tip of his napkin. *Strike one.*

Think of something else, Watkins. "What about school? You ready to go back?"

"Oh, yeah. I can hardly wait to graduate." She flipped her hair over her shoulder and watched the family beside them.

Strike two. This is like pulling teeth. She acts like I'm not even here. "Have you heard anything else from your job?"

"I go for a physical next week. If it goes well and my criminal record comes back clean, I'm hired."

"Uh-oh." Ryan tapped the top of her hand. "Your speeding tickets are going to come back to haunt you."

"I don't have any speeding tickets."

"I was just kidding."

"Oh."

Ryan sighed. *Strike three.* No doubt about it, he had struck out. They ordered their food and ate in near silence. Ryan watched Kylie focus on everyone in the restaurant except him. Something was wrong. Sure, Kylie hadn't sent tons of signals suggesting her interest in him, but she had shared her job offer with him first thing, even before she'd told Robin.

He smiled. "I've got an idea."

"Yes?"

Ryan furrowed his eyebrows. He hadn't meant to say that out loud. "When was the last time you went to Frosty's Fun Center?"

"Never."

"Never?"

She shook her head.

"Not even as a kid?"

Her expression clouded, and Ryan knew he'd said the wrong thing. He pulled cash for their dinner from his wallet and laid it on the table. "Well, I'm going to take you."

"I don't know. I'm a little tired."

"Come on, Ki."

A faint smile lifted her lips, and a glimmer shot through

her eyes. "Something about you calling me that. . ." She shook her head and waved her hand. "Never mind."

Aha. It was there. He hadn't imagined it. She was attracted to him. He just had to convince her to let it grow. "Come on. We won't stay long."

"Okay."

Ryan led her to the car, opened the door for her, then walked over to the driver's side. He slid inside and drove to Frosty's. "Arcade or miniature golf first?"

Kylie's tenseness seemed to fade. "I'm afraid I'll be terrible at either."

"That's okay." He grabbed her hand and squeezed. "I'll just rub your face in it every time I beat you."

Kylie's expression charged with competition. "I'm going to take you down, Ryan Watkins."

Ryan wiggled his eyebrows and winked. "Bring it on, Ki."

She hopped out of the car and raced to the front of the building. Ryan followed her inside. She pointed to the pinball machines. "Arcade first."

He purchased tokens and escorted her to a racing game. "Okay, you'll control one car. I'll control the other. We'll race around an obstacle course. Understand?"

Kylie lifted her eyebrows. "No speeding tickets?"

Ryan laughed. "Nope."

She batted her eyelashes. "Good. I don't want to risk my job, you know."

"Just play."

They raced, and Ryan beat her easily, even with his effort to let her catch him. "We can go on to miniature golf."

"Let's play again." Kylie's eyes lit with pleasure.

"I didn't know you were so competitive."

"I'll beat you yet."

They played again, and Ryan still beat her despite slowing down at many places.

"One more time."

Ryan chuckled. "Okay." The cars raced down the arcade freeway. He shifted his gears and turned his wheel with his car easily taking the lead. "Ready to call it quits?"

"Never." Kylie giggled, then leaned over and tickled his ribs.

"What are you doing?" He swerved and his car plunged into the guardrail.

Kylie's car moved slow and steady but stayed on course. He turned his around and hit the gas again. She leaned over and tickled him once more.

"Kylie!"

She laughed as her car passed the finish line first. "I won! I won!" She pumped her fist in the air.

Ryan growled and grabbed her waist, pulling her toward him. She lifted her gaze to meet his, and Ryan longed to lean down and kiss her lips. He grazed her cheek with the back of his hand, and her eyes closed for a brief moment.

"You cheated," he whispered as he lowered his lips toward hers.

A push from behind knocked him into her, severing the moment. "Sorry!" a boy yelled, as he chased another child to one of the games.

"Ready for me to beat you at miniature golf?" Kylie smiled like the Cheshire cat as she reached up and twirled the bottom of his hair with her fingers. Surprise welled in her eyes. "I can't believe—I'm sorry. . . . I've wanted to feel your hair—oh, my."

She turned away from him but not before he saw her neck and cheeks blaze red. He grabbed her hand. "Let's go play." He led her to the shack where they picked out their golf clubs and ball colors. She put her ball on the tee, and he strolled up behind her. "You can play with my hair anytime you like."

She gazed up at him and wrinkled her nose. "You're trying to break my concentration, aren't you?"

Ryan touched his chest and tilted his head as if he had been wounded. "The things you accuse me of. I'm hurt."

Kylie rolled her eyes and swung her club. The ball launched through the air and hit the green of the second hole. She covered her mouth. "I guess I hit it too hard."

"You think?" Ryan laughed. He retrieved her ball and showed her how to hit it. By the time they'd finished, Kylie had beaten him. They walked back to the car, and Ryan relished the great time they'd had.

"It was pretty hard playing bad enough to let me win, wasn't it?"

"I'd say."

Kylie giggled. "The mark of a true man." She laid both hands on her heart. "He lets the lady win."

"It's true." Ryan pulled into her apartment's parking lot and walked her to the front door. "I had a really good time, Ki."

Kylie closed her eyes. Her tense stance had returned. Ryan brushed a wisp of hair behind her shoulder. "I'd really like to do it again sometime."

"Ryan." He watched her take a few quick breaths. "We can't."

"Why?"

"I need. . ." She looked up but not at him. "I need more. I just want to be friends." She turned away, opened her door, and slipped inside.

Ryan looked at the front door knocker. *I should just barrel in there and tell her to quit being silly.* He stared at the rusty spot at the bottom of the brass knocker. *I could tell her I am able to support her and she'd never have to worry about money again.*

He shook his head and walked back to his car. "Then I'd never know if she wanted me for me." Sliding into the driver's seat, he hit the steering wheel. "Why is it always about money? First Vanessa. Now Kylie."

Ryan looked at the passenger's seat and thought of Kylie sitting there only moments before. He wanted Kylie. He needed her to want him, with or without his money.

eight

"Well, hello there, big sis." Kylie's twenty-year-old brother pulled her into the house and smothered her in a bear hug.

"You're not missing any meals are you, Dalton?" Kylie broke free and patted her brother's rounded gut.

A monster of a smile bowed his lips. "Nope. When Mama's not feeding me, Tanya is."

Kylie's mouth fell open. "Tanya? Little Tanya Burns?"

"The one and only."

"You two are seeing each other?"

"I bought her a ring."

"You're kidding."

"Nope." He laced his fingers through his jeans belt loops. "I'd imagine we'll all be married before you."

Kylie squinted her eyes. "That doesn't hurt my feelings. Are you still going to the technology school?"

"Nope. Got a job at the mine."

"Why?" She smacked her hip. "Why would you do that, Dalton? Just—just look at Daddy."

Dalton frowned. "Yeah. Look at Daddy. He's raised eight children. Every one of them loves the Lord. Every one of them watched him work hard—"

"Dalton, you know what I mean."

"Let me finish." He pointed to his chest. "We've watched him love our mama, watched him come home from a hard day and sit on the porch and play his guitar and sing hymns to us." He pointed toward her. "When are you going to figure out what's important, big sister?"

"You know he had to have wanted a better life, an easier

60

life. He's sick now, little brother." She clenched her teeth and stared at him for several moments. Finally she exhaled. "I didn't come here to fight."

"Dalton, did I hear the door?" Mama walked up behind him. She clapped her hands when Kylie peeked around her overgrown brother. "Kylie, come here, girl! How was your drive?" She opened her arms and wrapped Kylie in an embrace.

"Hi, Mama." Kylie kissed her mother's cheek. "It wasn't bad. Just took a little over an hour." As always, Mama's hair was rolled in a large knot on top of her head. It was as close to being a beehive as she could get it without it actually being one. Her bright blue eyes sparkled, overshadowing the wrinkles that lined her face. Mama wore the same type of outfit she always wore: a pair of stretch-waist jeans and a blouse with a big floral pattern.

"Get yourself in this house. We don't see enough of you. First you go off to college an hour away, then you get an apartment that's an hour from the college and still over an hour from your family." Mama grabbed her arm and pulled her farther into the living room. The same burnt orange couch and light brown, oversize chair sat upon the same dark brown, worn carpet. The same old cuckoo clock rested on the wall above the television. Everything was clean but as aged as her parents' anniversary, thirty years.

"How's Daddy feeling?"

"He has good days and bad days. The good news is his disability starts next month."

"It's about time. Where is he?"

"Taking a nap." She looked at Kylie. "How long are you staying?"

"I have to work tomorrow afternoon."

"I'll tell you what. Let's call your sisters and your brothers-in-law and get their families on over here for dinner. I'll fix some fried chicken, and we'll whip up some mashed potatoes and baked beans—"

"Mama, you know Kylie's nothing but a nuisance in the kitchen."

Kylie looked back, scrunched up her nose, and stuck out her tongue at her brother.

"Now, Dalton, don't go picking on Kylie. Why don't you call Tanya and have her come over, as well?" She opened the freezer and grabbed several packages of chicken. "Your daddy will be tickled pink to see all of us here when he wakes up."

Kylie wrinkled her nose when her mother handed her a ten-pound bag of potatoes and a paring knife. She hated peeling potatoes. Trudging to the trash can, she pulled it beside the table so she could throw the peels into it. "I can't wait, Mama."

Later, as Kylie placed the last dish on the dining room table, she had to admit helping Mama in the kitchen felt wonderful despite the nick on her thumb from cutting some apple slices and the cut on her finger from dicing the onion.

"You helped Mama with all of this?" Sabrina, Kylie's oldest sister, set up the card table for her three boys and Natalie's son.

"Yes, I did."

"I'm impressed." Natalie smiled. "We thought you were only good at schoolwork."

"Ha-ha. I'll have you know—"

"Is that my Kylie?" Daddy's deep voice sounded from just outside his bedroom door.

"Daddy!" Kylie ran and hugged him. "I've missed you."

"And I've missed you." He looked past her. "Looks like the whole family's here."

"Yep."

He turned his head and coughed several times. He looked back at her, then wrapped his arm around her shoulder. "Well, let's eat. I'm starved."

His cough and the weariness in his eyes tugged at her heartstrings. She loved her daddy and couldn't imagine life without him. Soon God would provide her with the income to help her parents.

As everyone gathered around the table, Kylie walked her father to his seat. Soon the adults settled at the big table, and the four grandchildren sat at the card table.

"Are you ready for me to bless the meal?" asked her father.

"Yes, Daddy, let's hurry it up." Twenty-one-year-old Amanda snorted. "After all, I *am* eating for three."

"What?" Mama stopped arranging the serving dishes to make room for the butter dish and gawked at her fourth child. "Did you say *three*?"

"Me and my big mouth." Amanda hit the table. "I wanted to surprise you guys after dinner."

Kylie watched as tears glistened in her daddy's eyes. "I remember when Chloe and Cameron were born." He looked at his youngest children, the twins. "We had the best times, didn't we Mama?"

"It was an adventure, that's for sure." Mama walked over to Amanda, patted her shoulder, and kissed the top of her head. "The Lord just keeps on blessing us."

Kylie placed her napkin on the table. "Excuse me."

"Are you okay?" Daddy's face was etched with concern.

"My stomach's just hurting a bit. Must have been all the taste testing Mama made me do." She tried to chuckle. "You all start without me."

Kylie shut the door to the bathroom and dropped onto the pink toilet seat. Same pink toilet. Same pink tub. Same pink sink. Same single bathroom. Nothing had changed. They didn't have the money to change any of it. She bit her lip and willed the tears to stay away.

How could her parents possibly be happy that Amanda was having twins? Her sister was a baby herself, a baby married to a coal miner. Natalie, pregnant with her second child, married to a coal truck driver. *At least Sabrina had the good sense to marry a man with a safe and stable job.* Although she wasn't sure if being a high-school principal was exactly safe, but at least it was stable, and he had a good income. One that provided consistently for his family.

She remembered her father coughing when he got up from his nap. Coughing again when he sat down for dinner. She didn't know how many more years she'd have with her father. All because of the coal mines. She hated the feast or famine they'd endured as a family at the hands of her daddy's employer. She hated seeing her daddy sick.

Two brothers-in-law working in the mines. Now, her flesh-and-blood brother would join them. One grandchild after another, and none of her sisters had an education above high school. Yet her parents, her sisters, her brothers—they all seemed content, happy.

She stood and stared at herself in the mirror. "Am I missing something here?"

Yes.

She squelched the answer that popped into her mind. Yes, she was missing something all right. She was missing the fact that no one in her family had a lick of sense. No one except her.

❧

Ryan gazed out the window of the airplane. Kylie's rejection of him had hurt more than he initially realized. Trying to escape, if only for a few days, Ryan had booked a flight to see his old friend in Alaska. He sucked in a deep breath and blew it out slowly, willing the Dramamine to kick in. Though he traveled by plane at least three times each year, flying still made him nervous.

He closed his eyes and leaned back in his seat. A vision of Kylie peering up at him at the arcade just before the boy ran into them filled his mind. He visualized lowering his lips to hers. They were soft and sweet beneath his.

His mind shifted to the remembrance of the pain in her eyes when she told him she needed more. More. Why did women always want more? Why couldn't they be content with love, with knowing a man cared about them?

He turned his head. He didn't care what women wanted. Only what Kylie wanted. His heart was filled to the brim and spilling over with her, and he couldn't stop the overflow. *I think I'm falling in love with her.*

Darkness surrounded him for a brief moment. He jolted at the voice of a woman instructing him to remain seated as the flight landed. He rubbed his eyes and looked at his watch. "Wow, I've been out for three hours." He smiled. Dramamine was God's gift to the fearful flyer.

The plane landed, and Ryan snatched his carry-on bag from the overhead compartment. Holding in a yawn, he made his way past the attendant and into the airport. He stopped at a coffee shop and bought an extra-large black java. After a few quick puffs to cool the coffee, he sucked down a large gulp.

He rented a pickup then headed for his hotel. After checking in, he drove to the Alaskan Logging Company. He yanked his cell phone from his pocket and dialed the owner's number.

"You don't get to surprise me this time, buddy."

Ryan snapped his phone shut and turned at the sound of Jim's voice behind him. "You take all the fun out of things, Jim." He grabbed Jim Thompson's hand and shook it as he patted his friend on the back. "How are you and your ladies doing?"

"Good. Callie's working part-time in a florist shop now that all three girls are in school. What about you?"

"I'm doing good."

"Any special lady in your life?"

Kylie's face popped into Ryan's mind. He swept the image away. "No."

"Wouldn't you say it's about time?" He punched Ryan's shoulder. "Aren't you pushing thirty?"

Ryan forced a laugh. "Yeah. I'm just waiting on God's timing."

"Maybe you just need to make a move to cooler climates." Jim nodded for Ryan to follow him into the office. "You know I would welcome your help here. Your dad was one of my uncle's best workers, and the machine you invented—why, production has nearly doubled in the last several years."

"I'm glad to hear it." Ryan settled into the plush couch that sat opposite Jim's desk. The phone rang.

"Just a sec, Ryan." He picked up the receiver and his pen at the same time. "Thompson." A grin lifted his mouth, and he laid down the pen. "Hey, doll, how's your day going?" Jim's attention stayed on his desk as he shook his head. "Sorry 'bout that, but don't worry. I'll be home at six, and I'll call them. No, you don't have to worry. I love you. I'll see you tonight."

Jim replaced the receiver, and Ryan started to stand. "I'll come back tomorrow. Sounds like you need to get home."

Jim shook his head and motioned for him to sit. "No. It's fine. Callie had to take the SUV to the shop. She feels like she's getting the runaround. She just needed to know I'd take care of it."

Jim's words echoed in Ryan's mind. Callie wanted security. Kylie wanted security. Maybe Kylie's wants were less about money and more about her need to feel cared for. Ryan would do anything to ensure that Kylie was safe and taken care of. Somehow he had to prove it to her.

Maybe I need to take Jim up on a job here. Maybe she needs to know that I go to work each day and come home each night. Help me, Lord. I love the freedom I have to serve You in any way You lead. Now that Kylie's entered my life, show me how I'm to follow.

❧

Having spent a never-ending dinner with her future supervisor, Kylie led Brad Dickson to the exit of Marinelli's. If she had to spend another moment listening to Brad praise himself for his business abilities or brag about the many women who fell at his feet, Kylie felt sure she would vomit. She glanced at her watch. *We've spent forty-five minutes in the restaurant—it seemed like hours.*

She looked back at Brad, noting his exquisite pinstriped navy suit, starched white shirt, and red, silk tie. A power outfit, for sure. She wondered what he thought of her not-so-elaborate attire of a good pair of khakis and a fitted sweater. She'd thought their dinner would be a get-to-know-each-other-a-bit kind of thing. Obviously, he'd expected something a bit more formal. She pushed open the door and walked outside.

"That was a quaint place. Do you go often?" Brad peered down at her with a condescending smirk plastered on his face.

She recognized the tone. His intent was to make her feel inferior. Marinelli's was beneath him. Well, where did the man usually eat? A five-star restaurant? She agreed with Gramps. Marinelli's had awesome Italian food.

"Yes. It's probably my favorite restaurant."

"Really?" He wrinkled his nose. "I'm surprised you would take your future boss to such a second-rate place. I thought the meat was overcooked, the noodles pasty, and the bread had hardly any garlic taste to it at all."

What an arrogant, self-righteous baboon! Okay, so he didn't like the place. But why act as if she'd purposely tried to displease her boss? Anger surged through her veins. Taking slow breaths, she remembered who dwelled within her heart. *Help me turn the other cheek, Lord.* She closed her eyes for the briefest of moments. God called His children to love, to tell others about Him. *You never said it would be easy. Give me patience with him, Lord.*

"Hi, Kylie." She turned at the sound of Gramps's voice beside her in the parking lot.

"Hello, Gramps." She hugged the older man, then nodded toward Brad. "Gramps, allow me to introduce you to Brad Dickson. He'll be my supervisor at Miller Enterprises."

"How do you do, Brad?" Gramps grabbed Brad's hand and shook it firmly, then pulled Kylie close and patted her back. "You've got a good one here."

"I couldn't agree more, Gramps." Brad's smug tone made Kylie want to punch him in the jaw. She couldn't fathom how she would stand working with him on a day-to-day basis.

Gramps leaned toward Kylie. "Did you see Elma's hair this morning at church?"

Kylie shook her head. She watched as Brad's eyebrows lifted in humor. He cupped his chin with his finger and thumb, then smirked at her and Ryan's grandfather.

"The woman's hair was pink! Silly woman can't make up her mind." Gramps chuckled and nudged her shoulder, knocking her back a step.

Ryan walked up beside them. A knot formed in Kylie's throat. She hadn't seen him in two weeks, and she'd missed him more than she expected. Heat rushed to her cheeks. She didn't want Ryan to think she was dating Brad. "Ryan." She touched his arm. "This is Brad Dickson. He's my future supervisor."

Hurt flickered in his eyes before he nodded to Brad and grabbed his hand. "Nice to meet you."

Brad lifted his nose and grunted an acknowledgment. He released Ryan's hand and wiped his palm on his pants. The unbelievable arrogance of the man! He was nothing like this in the interview. He had been kind, more than civil, but then Mr. Miller had been sitting there, as well. She looked up at him and willed her dinner to stay in her stomach. How would she make it through each day on the job?

❧

Ryan studied this Brad Dickson. The man's dark blond hair had been highlighted with lighter streaks. Clean-shaven and groomed to a tee, the man would definitely be considered good-looking. He walked behind Kylie with his nose so high in the air, Ryan wondered if he would trip from not watching where he was going. Ryan had seen men like this before. Power hungry. Their main objective was to make others feel of little worth. *So this is what Kylie wants in a man?*

He huffed as he followed Gramps into the restaurant. He'd missed Kylie something fierce the two weeks he'd spent in Alaska. However foolish he'd been when he fell head over heels for Vanessa, Ryan wouldn't make the same mistake again, even if it ripped his heart to pieces.

nine

Having spent the evening before preparing food for the singles' get-together, Kylie placed the bowl of spinach dip and the plate stacked with homemade bread on the cloth-covered table. Robin laid homemade macadamia nut cookies next to the other desserts. Scanning the recreation room, Kylie inhaled a long breath, then rubbed her hands together. Ryan was nowhere in sight. Surprised by how much she missed him, her heart plummeted at his absence. She hadn't seen him for two weeks—outside of their brief encounter at Marinelli's.

"It's a little sad, isn't it?" Robin whispered in her ear.

Kylie frowned, fearing Robin had read her thoughts about Ryan. "Sad?"

"Yeah, it's the last singles' get-together of the summer."

"Oh, yeah. I guess it's sad." Kylie searched her mind for something encouraging to say. "But it also means school is about to start."

"Yeah." Robin looked away. "That's true."

With the thought planted in her brain, a seed of happiness sprouted in Kylie's heart. "The sooner it starts, the sooner it's over with." She linked arms with Robin. "We'll get up in the morning, drive the one-hour commute to campus, hit the coffee shop for a cappuccino, then head to class."

"Uh, sure." Robin gently unlinked her arm and pointed to the man waving to them from the far corner. Robin's face lit up and she waved back. "There's Tyler. Come on."

The sprout of happiness withered in Kylie's chest. She'd hardly seen Robin in the last few months. "We could hang out together. Just you and me. Talk a bit."

70

Confusion wrapped Robin's features. "Without Tyler?"

"Well, we haven't seen much of each other."

"Um. . ." Kylie watched as Robin's face scrunched in uncertainty with how to respond.

Kylie swatted the air then pushed her friend in Tyler's direction. "No. You go on." She lifted her purse. "I think I'll freshen up in the rest room then grab a bite of all this good food."

"You sure?"

"Yeah. You go on."

"Okay, see you later."

Kylie watched as Robin walked away without so much as a backward glance. Sighing, Kylie made her way to the bathroom. So much of her life seemed to be changing. Getting rocky. Unstable. First, her daddy's illness. Then Dalton's engagement. Amanda's announcement of twins. Now Robin's dating. It made her feel out of control.

She laid her purse on the sink and rummaged through its contents. Finding her lipstick, she opened it and applied the watermelon color. She smacked her lips together. Ryan had been right where she needed him all summer. Consistent.

What am I thinking? Ryan was a grown man working at Holiday World. Sure, he was godly and generous and fun to be around, but when the electric bill came due or the pantry emptied—then what? He'd take a side job as a lifeguard at a pool? No, Ryan's picture would not be the one displayed in the dictionary beside the definition of "consistent."

And yet he was just that.

Trying to forget the thought, she leaned closer to the mirror and brushed away an eyelash that had fallen on her cheek. "I wonder where he's been."

She stood straighter and brushed invisible wrinkles from her sundress's hem. "Classes will soon begin. Life will go back to normal. I will not worry about Ryan Watkins." She squirted some blackberry-scented lotion into her palm and rubbed her hands together. "I'm going to mingle"—she zipped her purse shut and exited the restroom—"have a bit of fun, then head home and go to bed early before work tomorrow."

A purposeful bounce had formed in her step by the time she reached the recreation center. "Only two more weeks of work at Holiday World." She pushed open the door. A groan sounded from the other side. She gasped, covered her mouth, and peered around the door.

"Ryan!"

"You pack quite a punch." Ryan touched each side of his nose.

"I'm so sorry. What were you doing right behind the door?"

"Reaching for the handle."

Kylie grimaced and moved his hands from his face to see the damage. "I'm sorry. You're not bleeding. A little red, maybe."

He sniffed and wiggled his nose. "I'm fine. How are you doing, Ki?"

Flutters filled her belly when he shortened her name. Wow, she had missed him. "I'm good."

"How's Brad?"

She shrugged. Why would he ask her about Brad the Baboon? She almost chuckled aloud at the thought of the pet name she'd made up for the man. "Good, I guess."

Taking in his cool blue gaze and sun-kissed nose and cheeks, she acknowledged how cute this Richie Cunningham was to her, more attractive than she wanted to admit. "I haven't seen you at work."

"I had some other things I needed to get done."

She furrowed her brows. "Don't you. . .don't you need to work? I mean, you said you didn't have a day job." She swatted the air. "It's none of my business."

"You want to get some food?"

"Sure."

Ryan led her to the table. She picked up a plate and loaded it with country ham biscuits, potato chips, fruit salad, crackers and cheese dip, and an oversize double chocolate brownie. After grabbing a can of pop, she sat at a vacant round table. Ryan sat beside her. "You want me to bless our food?"

"Sure." She bowed her head and closed her eyes.

"Thank You for our food, Lord. Thank You for this time of fellowship. I pray You will draw us closer to You, that our lives will be filled with joy and contentment. Amen."

She looked up at him, then down at her plate. Was her life joyful? Could she say she felt contentment? The thought of working with Brad Dickson made her feel nauseous. Her brother barely grunted at her every time she called her parents' house. Robin was preoccupied with Tyler. "Joy" and "contentment" were not words she would choose to describe her life right now. She bit into her sandwich.

"Excuse me. Can we have your attention for a moment?"

Kylie turned at the sound of Tyler's voice. He stood in the middle of the room, with Robin holding tight to his side. An indeterminable queasiness overtook Kylie.

"Robin and I have an announcement to make."

"No," Kylie whispered and barely shook her head.

Tyler's bottom lip quivered. "God blessed me once with a wonderful wife. When Cheryl died, I thought my whole life belonged to my son and the youth." He peered at Robin, and tears filled his eyes.

"No, this is not happening." Kylie gripped her fork.

Robin pulled a tissue from her front pocket. She handed it to Tyler, leaned close, and whispered something in his ear, then kissed his cheek. Tyler continued, "Well, God had other plans."

Kylie's heart sped up. "No."

"He blessed me to love again." He gazed at Robin. "I'm

humbled and honored to share with you that Robin has agreed to be my wife."

Kylie smacked her fork on the table, stood, and started to walk away.

"Kylie." Ryan tried to grab her hand.

"No, Ryan." She pivoted and gawked at him. "She does things on a whim. She never thinks things through. She needs"—she smacked her hip for emphasis—"to finish school." She peered at the ceiling, nearly hidden by red and blue helium balloons. "Am I the only person on the planet who believes in being sensible?"

She turned and walked to the rest room. The words of Ryan's prayer flooded her mind. Everything about Robin exuded joy and contentment. She'd practically floated on clouds each time she was with Tyler.

Kylie made her way to the mirror in the ladies' room and peered at her reflection. "Everything's going wrong, Lord."

❧

Ryan waited at the end of the line of people that had formed to congratulate the newly engaged couple. Two weeks he'd spent away from Kylie. He'd purposefully tried to get the woman out of his mind, out of his heart. Time away would squelch his feelings. Seeing her with Brad and again tonight proved his plan hadn't worked. When his turn came, Ryan hugged Robin and shook Tyler's hand.

"Where's Kylie?" Robin leaned close and asked.

"In the rest room."

Robin turned toward her fiancé. "Tyler, I'll be right back." She yanked Ryan away from the crowd. "Let's talk."

"What is it?"

"Kylie."

"I think she feels you've moved too fast."

Robin bit her lip. "Look. I love Kylie. We've been the best of friends for as long as I can remember, but she has issues."

"Issues?" Ryan frowned. He knew she wanted a good job

and a steady husband and that being financially secure seemed to be the most important pursuit of her life.

"Not like that. She just can't loosen up. Can't trust. Can't let herself—she's just so worried about having the perfect life she can't see when God's best is right in front of her."

"What are you saying?"

Robin huffed. "You." She poked his shoulder. "You, Richie Cunningham, are perfect for her. She's so consumed with her perfect husband, perfect kids, perfect dog running along her perfect white picket fence, that she's blind to what God has provided that is actually perfect for her."

"Aren't you being a bit dramatic?"

"No, I'm not." She stomped her foot then giggled at her reaction. "I'm always dramatic, but that doesn't change what's going on with Kylie. Being poor as a girl and now with her dad fighting black lung, she needs to feel safe." Robin cocked her head and stared at him. "What do you do for income?"

Ryan's collar tightened around his neck as Robin's scrutinizing gaze peered into him. "I work at Holiday World."

"And that's all?"

"I'm a Santa at the mall in Evansville at Christmastime."

Robin raised her eyebrows.

Ryan cleared his throat. "That's all the work I do that comes with a paycheck."

"Hmm. I think there's more to it than you lead on." She pointed her finger at him. "Look, I don't want you to give up on her."

"What about Brad Dickson?"

"Brad?"

Ryan rolled his eyes. "The guy she's going to work with. The one who took her on a business dinner a few days ago. Mr. Clean-Cut, Nose-in-the-Air—"

"Wow. I think the green-eyed monster's been paying Mr. Watkins a visit."

"Humph."

"He sounds cute, though." She laughed and punched Ryan's shoulder again. "I'm just teasing. I haven't met this Brad Dickson."

"You haven't?"

"Nope, and she never talks about him."

"Do you talk to her much now that your schedule is full with Tyler and Bransom?"

"You got me there." Robin bit her lip thoughtfully. "Look. Don't give up on her, okay?"

"Who says I'm pursuing her?"

Robin snorted. "I've been preoccupied, but I'm not blind. It's obvious you like her. Pray she can see past her fears. She wants you. She just hasn't admitted it to herself yet."

Ryan watched as Robin scurried back to Tyler's side. *It's obvious I care about Kylie, huh? And Robin thinks she cares about me—just doesn't know it.* In his peripheral vision, he saw Kylie sit down at the table. She scooped some fruit salad on her fork and took a bite.

But what about Brad? Robin didn't have an answer for him—didn't even know who he was. He looked at Kylie. He longed for her to be his. No matter what he did, his attraction wouldn't dissipate, wouldn't even budge. He made his way toward her.

"Hey." Ryan sat beside her.

"Hey." She smiled at him, but he could see the hint of red around her slightly swollen eyelids. "Are you still going to Belize in January?"

Ryan lifted his eyebrows. Her question surprised him. "Yes. We have a meeting this Friday."

"You guys have fund-raisers and other things to raise the money to go, right?"

"Yeah."

"I'd like to go to the meeting."

"Sure. I can pick you up at seven."

"That would be great." Kylie stood and picked up her plate and cup. "I'm pretty tired. I think I'm going to head back to the apartment, but I'll see you then."

Stunned, Ryan sat as Kylie threw away her food then headed out the door. She hadn't congratulated Robin and Tyler. Sadness gleamed from her eyes. Robin was right. Brad wasn't the problem. Kylie needed to trust God with her future, with her family's future. Yes, everything would work out as soon as Kylie put her full trust in God.

ten

A few days later, Ryan walked Kylie to the front door of her apartment after another missions trip meeting. "School starts tomorrow, huh?"

"Yep."

"What did you think of the meeting?"

"I'm looking forward to the trip. I want to hold the babies." Her eyes flashed with excitement as a smile warmed her lips. Ryan found himself wanting to touch the dimple on her chin. It was the deepest he'd ever seen; yet it added the neatest beauty to her face.

"You'll make a beautiful baby-holder." Ryan's voice sounded huskier than he'd intended. He cleared his throat as Kylie's cheeks blazed pink.

She jingled her keys. "I'm thinking of making hair bows for the fund-raiser."

"That sounds great."

"It's a lot of money to raise."

"God always provides."

Kylie peered up at him. She studied him with an intensity that would make a bear cower back into the woods. "You really trust Him completely."

She hadn't asked, simply stated. Ryan swallowed, pondering if the declaration was accurate. Did he trust God? Completely? Kylie struggled with trust in poverty. What about his wealth? The greed and power that had filled Vanessa's eyes when she learned of his worth flooded his mind. He remembered the way she had spoken with disdain to his friends who had less. Since then, he hadn't been able to risk letting others know his true financial status. His intentions had been to live humbly, but had it really been for pride? "I—I try to trust Him."

Kylie touched his cheek. "I'm thankful for your faith." Before he could respond, she thrust her key into the doorknob, unlocked it, and scurried inside.

Humbled, Ryan walked back to his car, contemplating if he trusted his Lord as much as he thought.

❧

Kylie settled into the wooden school desk. Her drive had been a long and lonely one. She was thankful that Robin planned to stay in the apartment until the wedding and that Robin's uncle offered to let Kylie keep the apartment until she had graduated and was gainfully employed. But she still missed Robin. The semester just wouldn't be the same without her best friend.

She shuffled her folders, then placed all but the one she'd designated for the accounting course under her desk. Retrieving two pencils from her purse, she checked to make sure they were well sharpened. She pulled her schedule from her pocket. Only four classes this semester. Since she'd attended summer courses the first two years, Kylie was able to finish all necessary accounting content except this one fall semester class. The other three courses she took simply to keep her academic scholarship.

Ms. Jones. She read the instructor's name for the class. Kylie had heard wonderful things about the fairly young professor. According to the buzz on campus, Ms. Jones was dynamic and an out-of-the-box thinker, yet she stayed abreast of the current business expectations. Kylie bit the eraser of her pencil. *It seems I heard she was expecting.*

Kylie dropped her pencil when Professor Nickels trudged through the door. His salt-and-pepper hair, a mass of wiry curls, swayed with each step he took. "I know you're expecting Professor Jones."

Nickels plopped his briefcase on the teacher's desk. "I'm not looking forward to teaching this class any more than you're interested in taking it." He scanned the room. His gaze landed on Kylie. He scowled.

He jerked a stack of papers from his case and walked to one side of the room. "Professor Jones is having complications with her pregnancy." He counted students and syllabi, then handed several to the first person in each row. "So, I'm filling in."

A small, dark-haired lady raised her hand. "Will Ms. Jones and the baby be all right?"

"How would I know?" Professor Nickels shrugged and turned toward the chalkboard. "Look at page one in your syllabus. . . ."

Kylie slumped in her seat. Perfect. This was just great. This semester was supposed to be cake, and now she had Nickels to deal with—again. She frowned at the packet in front of her. Robin, her ever-consistent pick-me-up friend, wouldn't be keeping her company on the long drive to campus. She wouldn't be walking to the coffee shop with her each morning to encourage Kylie to make it through his class.

Robin's eyes had shone like emeralds when she'd returned from the singles' get-together just a few weeks before. Her countenance had been a mixture of adrenaline, bliss, and contentment. "I'm not going back." Robin's words echoed in Kylie's mind. . . .

"What? But you have to. You want to graduate. You want to get a good—"

"No, Kylie." Robin had rested her hand on top of Kylie's. "I never wanted it like you did. Don't you see? That's why I still don't have a major." She looked at the engagement ring on her finger, then back at Kylie. "I'm twenty-three years old. All I've ever wanted was to be a wife and mom. Think about it. When you wanted to play business, I wanted to play house. When you wanted to play school, I wanted to play house.

When you wanted to play store, I wanted to play—"

"House," Kylie finished.

"Yes. This is what I want. God has given me such peace, such confirmation. I want you to be happy for me." She grabbed Kylie in a hug. "And I want you to be my maid of honor."

Kylie had wiped away the threat of tears that filled her eyes. "Of course I'm happy, and I'd better be your maid of honor."

The chalk screeched against the board, and Kylie snapped from her reverie. She glanced at the syllabus on the desk of the guy sitting beside her. Nickels was on page five. She flipped her pages over. Gazing at his scoring guide, she cringed. To be able to graduate summa cum laude, with a 3.85 grade point average or better, she'd have to have a B in this class. *I can do it.*

She looked at her watch. Five more minutes. Her cell phone vibrated in her front pocket. Discreetly, she pulled it out, as no one ever called her during the day once school started. Her phone's display read her parents' number, and her heart plunged into her gut. Quickly, she gathered her things and slipped out of the room. *Please, God, let Daddy be okay.*

She pressed the button. "Hello?"

"Hi, honey," her mother's voice sounded over the line.

"What's wrong?"

"Nothing serious."

Kylie let out her breath. "Mama, you scared me to death. I was sitting in class, and I thought something happened to Daddy."

"I'm sorry. I thought your classes started next week."

"Mama." Kylie bit back her frustration.

"Listen, I do have something I want to tell you, something for you to pray about."

"Okay."

"The lady handling Daddy's disability claim called and said

there's been a bit of a delay. Seems his checks won't start for another couple months."

"Are you all going to be okay? Dalton and Gideon are still helping out, right?"

"Well, Dalton's had a bit of an injury."

Kylie's heart sped up. "At the mine?"

"No. Playing basketball with his buddies. Seems he went up for a block and fell on his foot and broke it."

"Oh, my."

"I want you to pray for us. God has always provided. In fact, I love to see how creative He can be. He's already blessed us in that Dalton's boss is holding his job, and your daddy is feeling quite well."

"I'll be praying, Mama."

"Oh, did I tell you Chloe was selected for some sort of special soccer team?"

"No."

"You know how that girl is always dribbling the ball around the house. Well, she's really pretty good. It's a lot of fun to watch her games."

"Maybe I can get down to see one."

"I hope so."

"I love you, Mama. Tell Daddy I love him."

"I will. I love you, too."

Kylie snapped her phone shut as the students exited the classroom. Professor Nickels trailed behind them. *I don't know what it will take, but I will get an A in his class. I'll make sure Miller Enterprises is happy to have selected me. They have to be. My family needs me.*

≈

"Here, Ryan." Gramps shoved several boxes into his hands. "Stack these cereal boxes on that far shelf."

"Yes, sir." Ryan clicked his heels and marched like a soldier toward his destination.

"When you're finished, I need you to stack these rice boxes beside them. I'll start setting the vegetable cans on this shelf."

Ryan saluted then picked up the rice. "Aye-aye, captain."

"All right now, smarty-britches, we only have fifteen minutes before God's Pantry opens."

Ryan stacked the fruit cans beside the vegetables. "All done. What do we do when they get here?"

"Just follow me at first. I'll show you." Gramps patted Ryan's back. "I'm glad you're here with me today."

"I am, too, Gramps."

Gramps walked over to the door and unlocked it. Already two women stood outside. He looked at Ryan. "The place is too small. We let one person at a time come in." He turned to the second woman. "We'll be with you in just a moment."

Ryan watched as Gramps took a pink slip from the first lady. Because people were referred from the health department and could only come twice a month, they had to bring a slip with them. Gramps checked it off and wrote her name in a ledger then pushed a grocery cart over to her.

"Come on." Gramps motioned for the lady to follow him. He handed her peanut butter, beans, and several other items. They reached the cereal, and Gramps let her pick three different kinds. Ryan noticed the woman never actually touched the foods.

"Do you go to church anywhere, miss?" Gramps asked, his voice tendered in a way Ryan seldom heard.

"Not really," the woman answered.

He placed a gallon of milk in the basket. "We'd love for you to visit our church."

"I don't know."

"Have you heard of Jesus?"

"Sorta." The woman stared at the items in the basket.

Gramps opened the freezer and let her pick three dessert items. Once finished, he transferred the food into bags. He pulled out a tract and one of their church pamphlets from his shirt pocket. "Miss, I'm glad you came today. I'd love to talk to you about Jesus anytime you'd like. I hope you'll consider visiting our church. You can sit with me and my grandson. Right, Ryan?"

"Yep."

"Thanks." The woman averted her eyes and picked up two bags. "I'll be right back."

"Ryan and I will help you out." Gramps lifted two bags, and Ryan grabbed the remaining three. They followed her to an aged Chrysler. Ryan noted two car seats in the back as they filled her trunk. Gramps slammed it shut and walked to the front of the car. "Remember what I said, and bring your babies."

The woman smiled slightly. "I don't know. Maybe." She slid into the driver's seat and stuck her head through the window. "Thanks, Mr. Watkins."

"I'll see ya." Gramps waved as she backed out of the parking lot.

"You know her?"

"I see her every two weeks. Have the same conversation. Get the same response. But one day. . ." Gramps lifted his finger in the air. "I believe we'll see her in church."

"Why didn't she touch any of the food?"

"Not allowed."

"Not allowed?"

"There's a lot of people in this county who benefit from God's Pantry, people who use it for what it's meant to be—help to those who need it." Gramps's face clouded. "But we still get a few who abuse it, who try to take more than we can supply. Because of them, the rules are strict."

Ryan watched the woman turn the corner. "It's worth it, isn't it, Gramps?"

"Helping others is always worth it, even if only one of ten had a true need. I'd rather err on the side of being taken advantage of than miss helping those who can't help themselves."

Ryan's thoughts drifted to Kylie. She didn't physically need food like those he'd see today, but she had other needs. She needed peace, needed the ability to completely trust God with her finances and her future.

Lord, everything in me wants to tell Kylie I can provide for her for the rest of her life, yet I'm afraid.

Ryan scratched his jaw. *Afraid? Of what?* He no longer believed Kylie to be a money-grubber. He didn't think she'd fall in love with him the moment she found out he could provide, yet he needed to know she'd love him for him, only him.

"Trust in the Lord with all your heart." Did he trust the Lord enough to share his secret with Kylie? He shook the thought away.

Instead, Ryan thought of her compassionate expression as she watched the Belize missions trip video. He remembered the concern etched on her face as she spoke of her family. He knew her pain with Robin's decision not to return to school was founded in care and worry for her friend. Kylie loved. There was no doubt in his mind that her heart was filled with a want to see those around her happy and at peace.

She just wants to control how they get it. Ryan sighed. Patience was not his strong suit. Loving Kylie required nothing less. "She wants control. I want her to give it up right now so I can tell her I'll provide for her and her family for the rest of our lives," he mumbled. "We're a great pair."

"What's that?"

"Nothing, I'm just mumbling to myself."

"Well, let's get on in there. We've got work to do."

Ryan smiled as he followed Gramps into the building. Though usually a bit rough around the edges, Gramps was sweet as sugar to the people he met at God's Pantry. This was Gramps's missions arena, and Ryan felt privileged to be a part of it.

❧

Kylie gazed at the two bridesmaid dress pictures Robin placed in front of her. "Which do you like better?"

"They both seem a bit warm."

"Well, yeah, it'll probably be cold in December."

"You're getting married in December? That's less than three months away."

"We don't want to wait. We want to spend Christmas as a family."

"Oh." Kylie stared at the pictures. "Either is fine with me."

The phone rang, and Robin hopped up. "I bet that's the florist."

Kylie turned away from the magazine. She didn't want to think about Robin's wedding. She didn't want to think about her injured brother, her sick father, or her younger sister pregnant with twins. She didn't want to think about why God seemed so distant despite her continual pleas for help.

"I'm doing the right things, Lord. I'm finishing school. I've already lined up a great job. I'm doing what is good. So, why am I so miserable?"

"What good is it for a man to gain the whole world, and yet lose or forfeit his very self?" Scripture from the pastor's sermon pierced her heart.

She huffed. "He was talking about those who don't know Christ. I know Jesus, and I love Him with my whole heart."

"Trust in the Lord with all your heart." One of her favorite Proverbs verses slipped into her mind.

"I do trust You, Lord." A weight fell on her shoulders and dropped harder into her chest. "At least, I try."

eleven

Kylie glared at the numbers before her. Professor Nickels had assigned a project that she'd almost finished. Except the numbers wouldn't match up. Grabbing her calculator, she typed in the first row and tallied them. She flipped through the pages of the project to be sure she'd deducted all expenses, then she tallied the second column. She slammed the calculator on the table. "I'm still $9.53 off!"

She raked her fingers through her hair then trudged to the refrigerator and grabbed a pop. Unscrewing the cap, she took a long drink then wiped her lips. "If it was off by a double zero number, I could find the mistake easily." She slunk back into her chair. "But this could take forever to find."

A knock sounded at the door, and Kylie glared at the clock. "Who could that be?" She walked over and peeked through the peephole. "Ryan?" She unbolted the door and opened it. "Hey."

"Ya ready?"

"Ready for what?"

"Ready for the missions meeting." He furrowed his eyebrows. "You didn't remember we had another meeting tonight, did you?"

Kylie smacked her hip. "I completely forgot. I'm working on this project for my accounting class."

"Oh."

"But. . ." Kylie slipped on a pair of flip-flops and grabbed her purse. "I could use a break." After stepping outside, she dug through her purse, found her keys, and dead-bolted the door.

She followed Ryan to his car and slid into the passenger's seat. As he pulled the car into traffic, Kylie opened the visor mirror to apply some lipstick. She gasped. "Ryan."

"What?"

"I'm a mess." She stared at her face, clear of all makeup, of all color. "I forgot I washed my face when I got home."

"I think you look pretty."

"Pretty! I'm a ghost. I can't go looking like this." She scoured her purse for some blush, some powder, anything. Nothing. She couldn't even find her lipstick.

Ryan pulled into the church's parking lot. He shut off the car and turned toward her. Placing one hand on hers, he cupped her chin with the other and turned her to face him. "You're beautiful, Ki."

The intensity of his voice gripped her. His gaze devoured every inch of her face. Her heart fluttered at his attraction, and she couldn't tear her gaze from him. Her eyes widened as he leaned closer. *He's going to kiss me.*

Excitement tingled through her veins. *I want him to kiss me.* She closed her eyes and lifted her chin.

He kissed her cheek.

Stunned and a bit disappointed, she opened her eyes as he reached for the door handle. His hand shook as he pushed the door open. *He wanted to kiss me.* The knowledge surged through her in a satisfaction she couldn't describe. *I wanted him to kiss me.*

Digesting the truth of it, Kylie slipped out of the car and followed Ryan into the church. "Tonight we're splitting into groups." Ryan didn't make eye contact with her. "One group is made of medical people. One of manual labor or repair people. And the last are those who are going as Bible school workers or general helpers. We'll go to that group."

"So, they break up to. . . ?"

"To talk about the items we need to collect for our specific purposes—so that we can plan what we want to do and how we want to go about doing it."

"Oh, okay."

Kylie found a seat in the already made circle beside a large woman with an infant on her lap. "Hi."

"So, what are you going to be doing in Belize?" the woman asked.

Kylie shrugged. "I don't have any special talents. I can hold a baby, though."

"Ya want to start now?" The woman's face broke into a large grin. "I'm supposed to be making coffee for the group, but my husband couldn't get off work in time to watch Suzanna."

"Sure." Kylie reached for the baby then turned Suzanna around to face her.

"My name's Candy." She pulled up the baby's falling shoe. Suzanna smiled up at Kylie. "I think she likes you. You'll do just fine."

Kylie peered down at the baby. "I have four nephews and three more babies on the way." Of course, Kylie had hardly ever held any of them. She'd been too busy to visit much. A pain stabbed her heart as Suzanna reached for her necklace. Sudden longing for her family nestled inside her as she inhaled the sweet scent that belonged only to babies.

"She's a cutie, isn't she?" Ryan sat beside her.

"Yes."

"She's such a blessing for Candy and her husband. They had five miscarriages. Candy couldn't seem to carry a baby to term."

"Really?" Kylie caressed the baby's soft, chubby hand.

"Yeah. Candy and Michael looked like the perfect couple. Great jobs. Nice home. Both loved the Lord. But they hurt on the inside because they wanted a child so badly."

"I'm happy God allowed Candy to have her."

"Suzanna's adopted."

"She is?"

"Yeah."

A man at the front of the circle motioned for the meeting to begin.

Ryan leaned over. "Sometimes God gives us a different route. It may not be the one we expect, but it's still perfect."

Kylie kissed Suzanna's cheek. She tried to focus on the plans the group started to make, but she hashed over Ryan's words in her mind. She'd marked her destination as a high-school teen. Mapped out the perfect route and followed it to exactness. She was sure God had guided her decisions. Logically—practically, her plan made sense.

She glanced at Ryan. Not only was he fun to be around, his heart was also big, so generous—she'd never met anyone like him. And integrity. He didn't kiss her when she gave him the chance. She knew he wanted to. Her destination—graduation and a good job—was so close, only months away. Studying Ryan, she knew her heart longed for a detour.

God, my route is a good one. I want to be able to help my family. Surely I am following Your will. She glanced down at the Suzanna. Her heart wasn't convinced. Even her mind couldn't form solid confirmation. And peace evaded her completely.

❧

Ryan stuck a french fry into his mouth, then swallowed a gulp of pop. "So, whaddya think about Belize?"

"I can't wait to go."

"I'm telling you, Ki, there is nothing better than to see those children's eyes light up when we come. They know we're bringing balloons and candy and toys, and they know more about Jesus than a lot of churchgoing adults I know."

"I don't think I could dress up like a clown or anything like that."

"Hold the babies, huh?"

"Yep." She grinned, and crimson flooded her cheeks and

neck. "Or help in any way I'm needed."

"You'll do wonderful taking care of babies." He thought of Suzanna, wiggling in her arms. Contentment had flooded her face, and for a moment, Ryan imagined Kylie holding their child, their daughter.

He longed to take Kylie in his arms. Before the meeting, he'd almost done it. She'd closed her eyes, welcomed his kiss. But she wasn't ready. He knew she wasn't. He didn't want to risk her shutting him out completely.

He shoved another fry into his mouth as Kylie nibbled on a piece of salad. They really were different. Kylie ate a chicken salad with light dressing while he devoured a hamburger and french fries drenched in ketchup. She was a classic beauty sitting with a Richie Cunningham look-alike. She was steady; he was fly-by-night. Quiet Kylie. Outgoing Ryan.

And yet, she was right.

Everything about her drew him, especially their differences. He just had to wait for her trust issues with God to be resolved. God, in His perfect, humorous way, chose to work on Ryan's lack of patience at the same time.

"Have you already raised the money for the trip?" Kylie's question interrupted his thoughts.

Now would be the perfect time to tell her the truth. Vanessa's face flooded his mind. The expensive outfit she'd bought and handed him the receipt for the day after he'd shared the truth with her. She'd fawned on him, tried to manipulate him, and his heart had shattered. *No, he couldn't tell Kylie. Not yet.* "Uh, I haven't raised any money."

"Well, what kinds of things can we do? I just don't know how I'll ever come up with enough."

"You know about the craft fair in early November. That always goes over well."

"Yes." Kylie twirled a piece of salad with her fork. "I'm making Christmas-colored hair bows for that, remember? Do we do anything else as a group?"

"A bake sale, I know."

"That sounds good." She pushed a cherry tomato to the side of her plate. "Money. It's a constant pain in my side."

"God always provides."

"Yes. That's true." Kylie pinned him with her gaze. "But it's a lot easier for some than others. Like you. How in the world do you work for an amusement park and not think anything about the cost of doing this type of thing?"

Tell her now. This is your chance. Trust God with her response. "Well, I—"

"Does your grandfather pay for it? I guess since you live in his house, you can save up or something. Are you still working at the park on weekends until it closes?"

She thinks I'm a moocher. I need to tell her right now. Ryan sat still, unsure how to say the truth. "Just spit it out," Gramps would tell him, but it wasn't that easy. He probably did appear irresponsible in her eyes. Jim's words about a woman needing to feel safe and settled replayed in his mind. "The truth is—"

"I'm sorry, Ryan." Kylie pushed her salad away. "That was so unkind of me. And not my business at all. I have a big project due and a test coming. Brad called last night wanting to have another 'getting acquainted' dinner. I—I think I'm just stressed. Could you take me home?"

Brad Dickson. Just the mention of his name sent a wave of revulsion through Ryan. He remembered the way Brad had looked at Kylie as if she were dessert after the main course. The man had been condescending and rude, but Ryan hadn't missed that Brad also viewed Kylie as a physical beauty. Ryan also recalled Kylie's kindness toward the snake. "Sure, I'll take you home."

Ryan drove back to her apartment. He watched as she went inside, waved hesitantly at him, then shut the door. He couldn't fault her for believing he depended on Gramps. In her eyes, he worked at Holiday World. Soon he'd be unemployed.

His heart stung at the thought of her feeling he took advantage of others, but he had to put his pride to the side, had to wait until she loved him for the man he was and no other reason. His ego had to step aside and wait.

He turned the ignition as thoughts of Vanessa and Brad whirled inside his mind. *Maybe it is about my pride—only in a different way.*

ﻱ

I'm such a jerk. Kylie flung herself onto her bed. *I can't believe I said those awful things.*

A tear slid down her cheek. How can I be so attracted to him? She cuddled her pillow. This is worse than falling for a man who works in the coal mines. Ryan doesn't even have a real job.

She allowed the spilling of tears. She needed a pity party. Ryan Watkins made no sense. Her love for him didn't either. She sat up. "I can't love him."

Her perfect job destination, her graduation route flooded her mind. She didn't want to take a fall-in-love-with-Ryan-Watkins detour. She'd end up worse than her twenty-one-year-old sister, Amanda, who was married to a coal miner and pregnant with twins.

A vision of herself barefoot and pregnant, kissing Ryan—clad in his Holiday World uniform—filled her mind. Gramps sat on the front porch holding a red-haired toddler while another child played at his feet.

God, that is not the detour You want me to take. I don't believe it. I won't.

twelve

Ryan held up the blond-haired fashion doll adorned in a pink princess dress. *Dana will love this.* He picked up the dark-haired male doll that wore a tuxedo and laid both in his cart. On Ryan's birthday his favorite present was to buy for his godchildren.

Moving down the aisle, he took in the massive assortment of dolls. *Little Heidi will want a baby.* He selected a box that advertised a doll that could eat and soil its diaper. *Yuck.* He laid it back down. Another boasted its doll could do flips. Ryan shook his head. *I want to get her something soft.* He moved down and found a baby that looked real, even had downy skin. *Perfect.* He placed it in the cart beside the fashion dolls. *One more stop.*

He strolled to electronics and chose a handheld car racing game. *I'm set.* Getting into the checkout line, he knew he had two more stops. One to a favorite local restaurant, and one to the mall. He paid for the toys, headed into parking lot, then loaded the car. He yanked out his cell phone and dialed Kylie's number.

"Hello." Her voice sounded light, happy.

"Hey, Ki."

"Um, hi." It changed to quiet, unsure. Ryan didn't know if that meant she didn't want to talk to him or if she still felt bad for what she'd said.

"Today's September twenty-first."

"You're right."

"It's my birthday."

"Happy birthday." Her sincerity sounded in the inflection of her voice. "How old are you?"

"Twenty-nine."

"No way."

"Yep."

"You're six years older than me."

"I'm older than a lot of people think."

"I just thought—I mean. . ."

Ryan wanted to groan. His age made her think him even more of a loser. "I was wondering," he interrupted before she said something they'd both regret, "if you would go out to dinner with me to celebrate."

"You really want me to?"

"Yep. Can you be ready in about three hours?"

"Sure."

"Okay, see you then." He snapped his phone shut, drove to the restaurant, and picked up a gift certificate for Neal and Melissa. Afterward, he made his way to the mall in Evansville. He finished at the service center then walked past a glass shop. From the window, he spotted a single, long-stemmed, yellow rose. He thought of Kylie.

What would she think if I bought her a small gift? The desire to buy her the rose grew. *It's my birthday. She can't say a thing.*

He smiled as he lifted it off the shelf and took it to the clerk. The college-aged woman rang up the price. "This is my favorite piece," she said as she wrapped it in tissue.

"It is?"

"Yeah. Yellow roses are my favorite. They mean peace and friendship."

"They do?"

The lady laughed. "I think so. I get the colors and their meanings all confused sometimes, but I'm almost positive I'm right."

Ryan laughed out loud. "We'll just say you are."

She put the wrapped rose in a bag and handed it to him. "I hope she likes it."

Ryan lifted his eyebrows. "I never said that this was for a woman."

"What man buys a rose for himself? At the very least it's for your mom."

Ryan laughed out loud again. "Not my mom, and I hope she likes it, too."

❧

"Kylie, this is Neal and Melissa Nelson."

Kylie offered her hand in greeting at Ryan's introduction. She skimmed the room, laden with aged furnishings. Three children sat on the floor beside an enormous, panting mutt.

Ryan leaned over and petted the dog's head. "This is Mutt."

Kylie didn't squelch her giggle in time.

Melissa shook her head. "The kids couldn't agree on a name, so we didn't give him one. Now he's just Mutt."

"It fits him well." Kylie bent down and petted the dog's head.

"Me." The youngest girl pointed to her chest.

Ryan grinned and tickled her chin. "This is Heidi. How old are you, Heidi?" She held up three fingers.

"You're a big girl," Kylie chimed in.

"I'm Dana." The older girl stood, grabbed the hem of her skirt, and twirled it back and forth. "I'm five, and I'm in kindergarten."

"Hello, Dana." Kylie turned toward the older boy. "And you are?"

"Evan." The preteen's cheeks turned scarlet as he grabbed her hand.

"It's nice to meet you." Kylie smiled then quietly clasped her hands in front of her. She had no idea why Ryan had brought her here. He said they were going to dinner for his birthday—not that she minded meeting this family. They were nice, but she didn't know what she was supposed to do.

"You're pretty." Dana grabbed a wisp of her hair and shoved it in her mouth.

"Thank you."

"Today is Neal and Melissa's thirteenth wedding anniversary."

"Lucky thirteen," Neal bellowed in an exasperated tone, then wrapped his arm around Melissa's shoulder.

"You're lucky I'm with you." Melissa poked him in the ribs.

"Yes, I am." Neal kissed her forehead.

Kylie smiled at their banter. Their love for one another was evident. She nudged Dana. "Are they always like this?"

Dana pursed her lips and shook her head. "Always."

They laughed at the seriousness in Dana's tone. Ryan smacked his thighs, then knelt eye-to-eye with Dana. "I have a surprise for you guys."

"Yea!" Dana jumped up and down, clapping her hands. Heidi watched and then mimicked her sister.

"Yes." Evan made a fist, pumping his elbow next to his side.

"I'll be right back. Kylie's going to help me."

Kylie followed him to the car. He popped the trunk, and she gasped at the gifts filling it. "All of those are for them?"

"Yep. It's the best birthday gift I could get."

Kylie studied Ryan as he placed several presents in her hands then filled his own. Her parents were generous. They'd give the shirts off their backs to help someone in need. She'd never met anyone as giving as they were. Until Ryan.

Speechless, she followed him inside and helped distribute the presents. She watched in awe as the children squealed over their toys and as tears filled Melissa's eyes when she opened the restaurant and mall gift certificates.

"When do you want me to come get the kids so you can go?"

Kylie's mouth dropped open. Ryan actually watched the children when they went for their date that he'd paid for. *He's perfect. He's sickeningly perfect, and he doesn't work.* Her gaze skimmed the room. *Who paid for these things?*

"Kylie, will you come, too?" Dana peered up at her with doe-like eyes.

"Uh. . ." She gazed at the urchin. She couldn't say no. "If Ryan is okay with it."

"You know I am." He smiled and grabbed her elbow. "Kylie and I better go. We're heading to dinner. How 'bout two weeks from Saturday?"

"Sounds good to me." Melissa wrapped Ryan up in a hug, then embraced Kylie as well.

They said good-bye and walked back to his car. Unable to speak, Kylie stared out the windshield as Ryan drove to the restaurant. Once there, he grabbed a small, white bag from the backseat. *Another surprise, I'm sure.* Kylie opened her door before Ryan could do it for her.

Once settled into the booth, Ryan asked, "What did you think about the Nelsons?"

"They're a lovely family."

"Melissa and I lived on the same street when I moved in with Gramps. She's a good five years older than me. Growing up, I always had a crush on her." He chuckled. "I'd follow her around, and she'd fuss and push me away."

"And you're still pining for her," Kylie teased.

Ryan threw back his head and laughed. "Not exactly. Oh, don't get me wrong, when they married on my sixteenth birthday, I felt as if she'd done it on purpose just to spite me."

"They seem to be very much in love."

"They are. I'm the children's godfather."

"That's really neat."

Kylie bit her lip when the waitress brought their pops. She felt comfortable with Ryan, yet weird at the same time. Physical, emotional, and spiritual attraction for him churned within her. Logic sent her mind into a tailspin.

"Ki, I have something for you."

"Ryan, it's your birthday and all you've done is buy for everyone else."

"I don't need anything, and this is more fun." He fumbled

with the bag. "I hope you like it."

"You shouldn't have bought me anything. I was so mean the last time I saw you." She clasped her hands in her lap. "You're too nice."

"Probably why I've never married. You know what they say—girls don't like the nice guys." He shoved the bag closer to her. "Please take it."

"Smart girls do like nice guys, and they marry them, too." Embarrassment filled her when the statement slipped from her lips then smacked Kylie in the face. Was integrity worth more than stability? What was wrong with wanting both? Kylie dismissed the questions and lifted the tissue-wrapped object from the bag. Gingerly, she pulled off the paper and gazed at a yellow glass rose. "It's beautiful."

"The clerk said it meant peace and friendship, but she wasn't sure."

Kylie noted the nervousness etched in his voice.

"Friends?" She gazed into his eyes, searching them for honesty.

"I was thinking more along the lines of peace."

He wanted more than friendship. The truth of it was written all over his face. She couldn't take it anymore. "Ryan, are you a drug dealer?"

His eyes bulged and he frowned. "No."

"Did you win the lottery?"

"Never played in my life."

"Is your grandfather some wealthy landowner or business-man or something?"

He scrunched up his nose. "He's a retired military man. What are you getting at?"

"Where do you get your money? You buy presents for entire families. You take me out to eat and never let me pay. I don't understand."

She trailed the rose with her fingertips. "I worked all

summer to pay for my gas and utilities and whatnot. I'm living off scholarships and loans, but for the life of me, I can't figure out what you're living off of."

Ryan took her hand. "Okay, the truth is—"

"Kylie, well, imagine seeing you here." Brad Dickson rubbed the top of her arm in a possessive, overly familiar manner. Kylie recoiled as Brad turned his attention to Ryan. "I forgot your name."

"Ryan Watkins." Ryan extended his hand to Brad, who acted as if he didn't notice and looked back at Kylie.

She swallowed, willing ugly, spiteful words away from her lips. She wanted to be a witness to the baboon. *Oh, God, help me see him as You do. Someone who needs You.* "Hello, Brad. Are you here with a date?"

"No. Business dinner." He touched her shoulder again, and Kylie shifted in her seat to make his hand fall. He looked at her in a way that made her feel uncomfortable. "Something I'm sure we'll have to do. . .often."

Ryan leaned across the table. "Well, Brad." His voice, laced with protection, sounded thick and strong. "We'll let you get back to your business."

Kylie gazed at Ryan. He'd always shown her nothing but respect. Even now he would allow nothing less from someone else. She looked back up at Brad. "Yes. I'll see you later."

Brad huffed and walked away without another word. Kylie smiled at Ryan. She couldn't deny it. She was falling for him, even without a job. "You were telling me that you weren't a drug dealer or a lottery winner or a—"

A shadow fell across Ryan's eyes. He shook his head. "I was just going to say God always provides."

"Yes, He does, but that still doesn't tell me how you bought all these things. Did someone give you money for your birthday?"

"Please, just believe me when I tell you I'm not a criminal.

My life is surrendered to God and His work."

Kylie peered into Ryan's eyes. She knew he spoke the truth, but it still didn't make sense. And in her thinking, things had to make sense.

≈

"I was going to tell her, God. It was right on the tip of my tongue when Brad Dickson interrupted us." Ryan walked in his front door and slammed it shut. "The way he looked at Kylie. God, how can she even speak to him? He's a snake."

"What?" Gramps walked into the room. "You saw a snake?"

"Sure did," Ryan growled under his breath then looked up at his grandfather. "No. There're no snakes out there."

"Good." Gramps shuddered. "I hate them slithering creatures."

Ryan laughed when Brad's face came to mind. "I'm not too fond of them, either."

thirteen

Kylie twirled her pencil as Professor Nickels passed out their graded exams. Though she'd studied for a solid day before, the test had been more difficult than she expected. Too much of her time over the last few weeks had been spent planning the Belize trip.

I know I did well on the essays. They were simple enough, but the multiple-choice section was killer, and it was worth half. Nickels passed by her the fourth time but still didn't give her the test. She laid her pencil down and bit her lip. There can't be that many left. He ambled toward her and finally laid her test facedown.

"I can handle a C," she whispered to herself. "My grades are high enough that I could still pull off the B." Closing her eyes, she turned the paper over. She peeked open one eye and shut it tight again. "No."

Flipping her test facedown again, she gazed at the board where Professor Nickels wrote the results of the test: 3 As. 4 Bs. 12 Cs. 8 Ds. 3 Fs. "It's not possible."

She turned it back over and stared at the oversize, red F. "There has to be some mistake." Skimming the first page, she hadn't missed any of the multiple-choice questions. She turned the page, noting two questions she'd missed. The third page revealed one wrong answer. She flipped to the essay questions. In bright red, the words "Answer irrelevant to question" screamed at her. "Lacks supporting details" blared from the next essay.

"He's failed me on my essays." She scoured the questions and her answers to both. Digging through her folder, she found the notes she'd taken applying to both questions. "These are good answers. Solid."

Through her peripheral vision, she saw fellow students leave their seats. Nickels must have dismissed class, but Kylie couldn't move. She yanked her calculator from her purse and tallied her grades. An F on this test gave her a high C in the class. It wasn't possible. It wasn't fair. Her answers were well thought out, well written. Nickels had some sort of vendetta against her that she didn't understand.

A briefcase shut, drawing her attention. Nickels walked toward the door. *I have to talk to him about this.* She swallowed, dreading any kind of confrontation.

"Professor Nickels." She stood and met him by the door. "Can I ask you about my test?"

"I wouldn't be able to say if you can."

Kylie sighed, feeling as if her second-grade teacher had just reprimanded her. "May I speak with you about my test?"

He nodded. "Yes, you may."

"I don't understand why my essay grades are so low." She pulled out her notes. "My answers look very much like the notes I took from your presentation."

"You didn't explain yourself well. Look." He pointed to his personal scribbling. "I told you, you lacked details."

Kylie cleared her throat. She had no intention of being disrespectful, but something wasn't right. He'd taken too many points away. "Professor Nickels, you gave me almost no points, and I identified each area with a minimum of a paragraph of explanation."

"I can't help it that you have poor writing skills. I could not make heads or tails of your support. Besides, essays are subjective."

Kylie gawked at him. It was personal. There was nothing she could say to him, probably nothing she could do to get the grade she needed from this class, except go to administration.

She wasn't sure she had the desire to do that. "I'm sorry I took up your time." Kylie headed out the door.

"I hear you have an offer from Miller Enterprises."

Kylie turned on her heel. "Yes, I do."

"That's quite an accomplishment for a soon-to-be grad. Most new accountants start out working for a small business, doing some income tax work and whatnot. Miller handles several upstanding business accounts."

"I agree. It's my dream job."

He lowered his head, peering at her from above his bifocals. "You're not ready for that."

Kylie straightened her shoulders. "I will work hard for them. Give my best."

"Hard work is a good thing, but you don't have what it takes, Kylie Andrews."

Kylie stared at him. His disdain evident, she had no idea what caused it. "I hope your personal beliefs have nothing to do with my grade."

He lifted his head and pushed his glasses up on his nose.

Kylie pivoted toward the door. "I'll see you Monday, Professor Nickels."

❧

"I've never seen you two before. Are you new to the community?" Gramps asked the older woman and young, pregnant lady as Ryan placed canned beans in the cart.

"We're not really from around here—a county over. My husband worked in the coal mines. He's gotten sick with black lung. His disability will start in a month or so, but we need to take what the Good Lord provides until it starts."

Ryan took in the woman's salt-and-pepper hair. Her skin was wrinkled from age and what he suspected to be a hard life, but her eyes shone with laughter and happiness.

"I'm just here to help Mama." The obviously pregnant younger woman smiled. Her light-colored, straight hair reminded Ryan of Kylie's. Her eyes kind of did, as well.

"Well, we're glad to help," said Gramps. "How is your husband?"

"He's doing well. Rests quite a bit but picks up his energy whenever the grandbabies come around."

"How many grandbabies do you have?"

"We have four grandsons and three babies on the way. Amanda, here, is giving us twins." She laughed and her face lit up. "I'm hoping for at least one granddaughter. I'm anxious to buy a dress or two."

"Sounds like you have a wonderful family." Gramps pushed the cart toward the refrigerated items.

"Oh yes, Jesus blessed us with eight children, and every one of them is serving Him."

Ryan perked up. *Eight children? And this pregnant lady looks a lot like Kylie.*

The woman continued, "My third daughter is getting ready to graduate from the University of Evansville, then she's heading on a missions trip in January."

Gramps smiled. "My grandson is going to Belize in January."

The woman peered up at Ryan. "Belize is where my girl is going."

Ryan cleared his throat. "What did you say your name was, ma'am?"

"I'm Lorma Andrews. This is my daughter, Amanda."

"Andrews?" Gramps smacked the counter and grinned. "Is your daughter Kylie?"

"Yes."

"Well, it's a small world after all. Ryan and I know Kylie. She's been going to our church since she and her friend moved near Santa Claus. We've had dinner with her a few times. Ryan worked with her at Holiday World." He looked at Ryan and winked. "Special girl, wouldn't you say?"

"Are you Ryan Watkins?" asked Amanda.

A shot of excitement zipped through his veins. Kylie had talked to her family about him. "Yes."

"You're the Ryan my Kylie talked about?" Lorma Andrews poked Amanda's arm. "What time is it, dear?"

"Eleven thirty."

"Amanda and I brought some lunch for the trip over here. I'd love it if you two would join us."

"We've got turkey and ham sandwiches, potato chips, and sliced veggies. Pickles and homemade chocolate cake, too," Amanda added.

Gramps rubbed his stomach. "Sounds wonderful. We'll be happy to join you, but our lunch doesn't start until twelve."

"That'll be fine. Amanda and I will get it all set up on that picnic table I saw around back."

Ryan carried the cooler to the table for Mrs. Andrews and Amanda to set up their lunch, then he busied himself with stocking the shelves and breaking down boxes. Half an hour seemed to never pass. He could hardly wait to learn more about Kylie's family.

At twelve exactly, Ryan and Gramps headed out to the picnic table. Ryan filled his plate then bit into his sandwich. "This is wonderful."

Gramps wiped his mouth. "Best lunch we've had in a while."

"Thank you." Mrs. Andrews smiled then took a bite of her pickle.

Gramps elbowed Ryan then cleared his throat. "Ryan and I adore Kylie. Tell us about your family."

"Well, my oldest is Sabrina. She's married to our high-school principal. They have three sons. Next is Natalie. Husband's a coal truck driver. They have a son and another on the way. Then there's Kylie. Then Amanda here, whose husband works in the coal mines, too. I told you she's having twins. Next is our first boy."

She laughed. "Took us five times to get us a son; now I can't seem to get any granddaughters. Anyway, Dalton's next. He and Kylie love to argue. When they were little they'd wrestle around on the floor until something was broke or spilled."

Her eyes glazed at the memories. "Then we have Gideon. He's getting ready to go to Indiana University; wants to work in agriculture. Last, we have the twins, Cameron and Chloe. Chloe might as well have been a boy. She loves to run and tumble and fight with them. I guess that's what happens when your sisters are all several years older and your brothers are about the same age. She was just selected to a special soccer team."

"Sounds like a lot of fun." Ryan raked his fingers through his hair. "I didn't have any brothers or sisters."

"God blessed us with a full home." She patted Ryan's hand. "Maybe He'll give you a passel of kids of your own to raise someday."

Ryan envisioned several stair-stepped, blond-haired girls and boys scampering around his front porch. Kylie sat in a rocking chair, cuddling another over her shoulder. His heart warmed. "Maybe."

They continued to share until it was time for Gramps and Ryan to reopen God's Pantry. Mrs. Andrews walked around the picnic table and wrapped Ryan in an embrace. "It was nice to meet you. I need you to do me a favor."

"Sure."

"Don't tell Kylie we were here. She worries herself sick over her daddy and me. I try to tell her God always provides, but Kylie's a fixer. She loves Jesus with all her heart, but she wants to take care of things."

"Yes, I know."

"I bet you do." Lorma Andrews studied him for a moment then patted his hand. "Hang in there. We're praying."

᠔

Robin flipped through pages of the bridal magazine. "You know you could complain to administration."

"I know." Kylie replayed Professor Nickels's words in her mind. He said what she'd been feeling—*"not ready."* All through college she'd been on fire to get her degree—single-minded, focused. Now she was confused. Her passion had waned. She felt drawn to something different.

Gazing at Robin as she wrote down different menu options, Kylie picked up her test once more and scowled at it. "I'm just tired because the end is getting close."

Robin slipped out a photo from inside her purse. "Look, I took a picture of Bransom in the tux he's going to wear."

Kylie grinned at the small, dark-haired boy who looked so much like Tyler. Robin knelt beside him with one arm around him and both hands cupping his shoulders. His head was tilted as he focused on his soon-to-be mother. The image tugged at Kylie's heartstrings.

She knew her pursuit to get her degree was a good one. Her heart had been in the right place—at least she thought it had been. But that little slip of paper from the University of Evansville had been her sole purpose for more than three years. Lately, she longed for more.

"He's adorable, Robin." She handed the photo back to her friend. She lifted her exam. "I'm going to put this away and get my pj's on."

Once in her room, Kylie plopped the exam on her dresser and knelt next to her bed. "God, I'm confused. I can hardly fathom that I've spent this long doing the wrong thing when I've always tried to seek You. But it's Your will I want, not my own. Show me, Jesus. Give me strength no matter what that means."

Her cell phone rang. Kylie picked it up and read Candy's number in the window. She pushed the TALK button. "Hello."

"Hi, Kylie," Candy's voice sang over the line. "I wanted to ask you about interviewing for the missions ministry position."

"There's a missions ministry position?"

"It's going to be a new job—the only paid position the ministry will have. Whoever gets the job will keep track of missions trip dates, the travel fares, the accommodations, and other stuff. He or she will keep the books, as well as stay on top of what needs to be bought or collected from different churches or locations, keep up with volunteers—just a whole bunch of stuff."

Kylie bit her bottom lip. "It sounds interesting." She and Robin had only joined the church as members about a month ago, and now she was being asked to interview for a paying position.

"And you'd be more than qualified. . . ."

fourteen

Kylie had no idea what she was doing. After walking into Candy's family room, she peeked around the dining room door and saw all five of the missions ministry's leaders sitting in a semicircle around a lone chair. Hers, she presumed. They chatted amongst themselves and hadn't realized she'd arrived. "I'm so glad you accepted the interview," Candy whispered behind her.

"I can't believe I'm here," Kylie whispered to her new friend. Baby Suzanna cackled and kicked her legs. Kylie tickled the baby's chin and heightened her voice. "I've already got a job, don't I, Suzanna? Yes, I do."

Suzanna wiggled in her mother's arms, and Candy kissed her head. "Sometimes what we think we're supposed to have isn't what's meant for us at all. God has a different plan."

Kylie took a deep breath. "That's what Ryan said when he told me about you and Michael adopting Suzanna."

"You know, if we'd had a biological child, we probably would have never gotten Suzanna." She cradled the child closer to her chest. "And what a blessing we would have missed."

Kylie allowed Candy's words to seep into her heart. *Ryan.* The man had infiltrated her every waking, even sometimes sleeping, thoughts. He touched her to the very core of her being. She adored him. Heat rushed to her cheeks as she remembered how she'd drilled him about money at dinner the other night. She didn't understand it, and she needed to—desperately. Her head had to believe he could provide for her, because her heart didn't seem to care.

Clearing her mind, she pushed the dining room door open all the way and walked inside. She nodded at the ministry leaders and sat in her seat. "It's nice to see you all today."

Pastor Chambers smiled and scratched his nose. "We're glad you're here." He leaned back in his chair and drummed his fingers across his potbelly. The vision almost sent Kylie into a fit of giggles—she'd watched her pregnant sisters do the same thing. "Kylie, we understand you've already been offered a position at Miller Enterprises."

"Yes, that's true." *And it's a great position,* she wanted to add. Any accounting major would be ecstatic knowing Mr. Miller had even looked at his or her résumé and overwhelmed to be considered for an interview, but to actually get the job? It was unheard-of.

"But you're willing to consider interviewing with us?" asked Pastor Foster. He pressed his fingers against his overgrown eyebrows. Being color-blind and unmarried, Pastor Foster's clothes rarely coordinated. Today was no different. He wore a pair of khaki-colored dress slacks, a nearly lime green dress shirt, and a deep red tie with a black paisley design. Sometimes she thought he mismatched his clothes on purpose as a means to get people look at him, at which point he'd run up and introduce himself. She loved his personality, the way he didn't mind what people thought of his appearance.

She crossed her legs. "I guess I am willing to interview. I'll be honest with you; I'm not sure why I accepted. The position at Miller Enterprises is one I've always wanted." She uncrossed her legs and flattened her hands against her thighs. She didn't want to sound ungrateful, but she wanted to be truthful. It wouldn't make any sense for her to take a different job offer. She looked at the leaders sitting across from her. "When Candy asked me to come, I—I just felt I should."

Pastor Chambers bent over and picked up a folder. "We'll level with you. This is a full-time position, but the pay is probably substantially less than what you've been offered. Volunteers have kept the business and accounting aspects of our missions running, but it's becoming too big of a job." He handed her the folder. "Look it over."

Kylie opened it and looked at the job's duties. Everything seemed within reason. In fact, she wondered if the position really would require a forty-hour workweek. She flipped the page to find the salary and benefits. It was almost half what she'd been offered from Miller.

The logical response was to decline. Now. Before she left. Before she even got up from her seat. Yet, she paused. The income was enough for her to live modestly, and she'd have time to spend with her family. She longed to see them more, to hold her nephews and maybe one day soon her nieces, to cherish the last bit of time she'd have with her daddy. The last few family get-togethers they'd shared had been a lot of fun. She felt close to her siblings again, in the same way she had when they were little.

Looking up at the ministry leaders, she thought of how easy it would be to work with these men and women. Ease at the office was not something she expected at Miller's. She shut the folder and held it to her chest. "May I pray about this for a few days?"

Pastor Chambers grinned. "Absolutely. You didn't join our church until God showed you the time was right." He paused. "Tell you what. I'll give you a call in two weeks. We're not in a rush, and we want you to be sure of your decision."

"Thank you."

&

Glad Kylie had agreed to go with him to help take care of his godchildren while their parents went on their date, Ryan glanced at Kylie in the passenger seat then looked in the rearview mirror at Evan, Dana, and Heidi. Kylie had no idea what he had planned for the day. Simply telling her to wear tennis shoes and something comfortable for outside, he'd hoped it would be a surprise for her as well as the kids. Now he wasn't sure he should have kept it a secret. The day would be quite eventful—and exhausting.

He turned onto the road leading to Holiday World. Signs greeted them from every side. Kylie looked at him. "Are we—"

"We're going to Holiday World!" Evan shouted from the backseat. "Ryan, thank you, thank you, thank you."

"I've never been to Holiday World." Dana's eyes grew big with excitement. "Mommy said I'll get to go one day soon enough, when I'm in fifth grade. That's when the school—"

"What Howiday Word?" Heidi asked from the backseat.

Ryan pulled into the parking lot and turned off the car. He turned toward Kylie. "Are you okay with this?"

A full grin lit her face. "This will be great."

Relief flooded his heart as he turned toward the children. "Now, you know it's October. That means Splashin' Safari is closed."

"What Spashin' Sari?" Heidi asked.

Evan leaned toward her. "The water rides."

Ryan nodded. "Yes, but we'll still be able to get on the other rides."

They filed out of the car and walked toward the entrance. Through peripheral vision, Ryan watched as Kylie scooped Heidi into her arms so the girl wouldn't have to walk as far. *I never even thought of bringing a stroller. We'll just rent one.*

"Can we ride the Raven first?" Evan rubbed his hands together as they entered the park.

"What's the Raven?" asked Dana.

"It's the best roller coaster in the whole world," Evan proclaimed. "Can we?"

"That sounds fine with me. First, let's rent a stroller." Ryan looked at Kylie. She smiled and nodded in agreement.

Moments later, Kylie strapped Heidi into her stroller, and

they headed toward the roller coaster.

"Look." Dana pointed toward the dog character with HOLIDAY WORLD written on his chest and on a blue cap that sat on his head. She clutched Ryan's hand.

"That's the park's mascot. His name is Holidog. You want to go say hello to him?"

Dana's voice quieted. "I—I guess."

Ryan motioned for Holidog. As the character ambled closer, Heidi broke out into screams of terror. Stunned, Ryan watched as Kylie turned her away and unbuckled her from the stroller. Within a moment, Kylie had Heidi out and nestled against her chest. Kylie whispered quiet words of comfort to the child.

Dana gripped Ryan's hand and half hid behind his leg. He hadn't been prepared for this. Evan saved him when he shook Holidog's hand and said, "See, Dana. See, Heidi. He's nice."

A hesitant smile lifted Dana's lips as she gripped Ryan's leg with one hand and shook Holidog's hand with the other.

"You want to say hi?" Kylie asked Heidi, but the child shook her head and wrapped her arms around Kylie's neck. "Okay." Kylie's voice was soothing as she stroked Heidi's hair. "That's okay. You can stay right here with me."

Ryan's heart nearly burst with adoration for the woman as they walked away. She knew exactly what to say, what to do to calm Heidi. A natural love for his godchild spilled from within her. She'd make a wonderful mother.

The hours passed, and Kylie still held Heidi everywhere they went. The poor child was completely overwhelmed by all there was to do and see at Holiday World. Dana relished riding the Hallow Swings. Evan had even convinced her to ride the Legend roller coaster as she just made the height cutoff, but Heidi remained as close to Kylie as her little body could get. After enjoying pizza for dinner, Ryan took them to the souvenir shop and let the children pick out a candy and toy. To his surprise, Heidi selected a stuffed Holidog. She gripped it in her hand and nestled back into Kylie's chest.

Walking back to the car, Ryan wondered what Kylie thought. She had to be exhausted. Heidi wouldn't let him take her, though he'd tried many times. He knew Kylie's arms had to ache. After Evan helped secure Dana's seat belt then latched his own, Ryan watched as Kylie lowered Heidi into her car seat and fastened it. Kylie slid into the passenger seat, laid her head back, and closed her eyes. *What was I thinking taking the children to Holiday World? I've worn Kylie to the bone. She'll never want to do anything like this again.*

He drove to the Nelsons' house and stopped the car. Evan and Dana jumped out of the back and raced inside, yelling about the great day they'd had. Kylie stepped out of the car and unbuckled a sleeping Heidi. She picked her up and nestled the girl into her shoulder. After kissing her cheek, she handed Heidi to Melissa, then got back into the car.

"Thanks for taking them." Melissa smiled at Ryan.

"Did you and Neal have fun?"

"We had a great time. You're too good, Ryan Watkins." She kissed his cheek. "I better take this girl inside. She's plumb tuckered out."

"Yes, she is." Ryan got into the car. He looked at Kylie. *That one is plumb tuckered out, too.* He drove to her apartment. Silence filled the car. Peeking at her, he noticed her head resting against the window, her eyes closed. *I've killed her, Lord. I should have told her my plans, given her the chance to say it would be too hard of a day.* He pulled into the parking space and turned off the car.

He gently touched her cheek. "We're here, Ki."

Her eyes fluttered open and she inhaled a long breath. "I'm sorry. I must have fallen asleep."

"No, I'm sorry. I should have told you where we were going. I never dreamed Heidi would—"

Kylie placed her hand on his. A single tear slipped down her cheek. "That was the best day I've had in a long time. Thank you for taking me."

Stunned, Ryan watched as she opened the door and made her way to her apartment. She waved and then slipped inside and shut the door.

❧

Kylie fell onto the couch in utter exhaustion. She allowed the tears to fall down her cheeks as the sweet smell of Heidi lingered about her. She could still feel the girl's embrace about her neck. Probably had the marks to prove it. *God, I've missed so much with my family, with my own nephews. I've been so preoccupied. Give me the chance to love on them. To go to the park. To read them a story. To hold them and tell them how much they mean to me.*

The folder from the ministry leaders lay on the coffee table in front of her. Her heart screamed to take the position. She'd have time to spend with her family, but what about Miller Enterprises? It was her dream, her means to help her family. Surely it was God Himself who'd provided her with the position. She sat up and kicked off her shoes. Yes, she was just being emotional. She was tired from the long day. Without a doubt, God had blessed her with a wonderful opportunity and the perfect job.

fifteen

After several knocks, Kylie opened the front door. Wearing a pinstriped brown suit and yellow silk tie, Brad smiled down at her. She'd pegged him sly as a fox, but there was no denying he'd been hit by the handsome stick.

"Kylie, you look surprised to see me."

"I am. You know where I live?"

Brad smirked. "It would be on the résumé." His gaze roamed up and down her body. "Cleaning today?"

Feeling violated, Kylie squinted as her lips formed a straight line. She tugged the bottom of her white T-shirt farther down her jean shorts. "No. As a matter of fact, I'm getting ready to go to an *informal meeting.*"

" 'Informal' being the key word." He snorted and tilted his head to look past her and into her apartment. "Good manners would insist you invite me in."

"No." Kylie stepped outside and shut the door behind her. "Not necessarily. Especially not when the weather is as lovely as it is right now and we have two comfortable chairs to sit in and enjoy it." Kylie sat in one of the lawn chairs on the apartment's small front porch. She motioned for Brad to sit in the other. "Now, to what do I owe the privilege of this visit?"

He dusted the chair's seat, then sat. "All right then." He clasped his hands. "Miller's been trying to get in touch with you for a week."

"He has? My answering machine's been giving me fits. One moment it works, the next it doesn't."

"Well, he planned to cancel a meeting to make a trip over here, but I told him not to worry. I could handle this."

Queasiness churned inside her. "What's up?"

He handed her a memo. "It seems the position you were hired for isn't needed."

Kylie tried to skim the content. Heaviness filled her heart, and tears welled in her eyes. She took long breaths to hold her emotions at bay in front of Brad. Standing, she lifted her chin and extended her hand. "Thank you for coming personally."

He stood and took her hand. "That's the breaks, kid." He winked, turned, and walked toward his car.

Kylie stepped inside the apartment. After shutting the door, she leaned against it and allowed the dam inside her to crumble. *I guess You're telling me to take the job at the ministry, God. I thought I was keeping the one at Miller's.*

❧

Arms full of Chinese takeout, Ryan kicked Kylie's front door with his foot. His heart had plunged when she'd called him crying, saying she couldn't attend the missions meeting. He couldn't make heads or tails of her reason. He could only distinguish the word "Brad."

If there was a person on the planet Ryan felt distrust for, it would be Brad Dickson. Christian feelings did not surface when Ryan thought of that man. The fact that Brad often sweet-talked Kylie didn't help matters.

Kylie opened the door. Her eyes, bloodshot and swollen from crying, glanced at his packages. She sniffed and offered a weak smile. "Come on in, Ryan."

He set the bags on the table, then pulled out a box. "I've got sweet-and-sour chicken, sweet-and-sour pork, some General Tso's, two kinds of rice, crab rangoons. . ."

Kylie rested her hand on his. "Thanks, Ryan." She disappeared into the kitchen and returned with two plates, forks, and cans of pop. They filled their plates. "Let's go sit on the couch."

Ryan picked up his drink with his free hand and followed

Kylie. They ate in silence except for Kylie's occasional sniff. Ryan peeked at her, unsure what to say and when to say it. He took another bite and swallowed. She sniffed. He couldn't take it anymore. "You want to talk about it, Ki?"

She let out a long breath. "I don't have a job in January."

Ryan laid his plate on the coffee table and scooted closer to her. He wrapped his arm around her shoulder. "I'm sorry."

Tears formed and spilled quickly from her eyes. "It was the perfect job, and Miller sent Brad over here to tell me. Mr. Hoity-Toity himself."

"I thought you liked Brad."

Kylie scrunched up her face. "Ugh. He's an uppity snob if ever there was one." Kylie's expression loosened. "I shouldn't have said that. I try to pray for him. He just makes me so—so mad."

Ryan scratched his jaw. Here, he'd believed Kylie liked Brad, but if he thought about it, Kylie never flirted. She was polite, courteous, but she didn't lead Brad on. He peered at the woman beside him. She wasn't like Brad or Vanessa. She was goal-driven, determined, but she wasn't money hungry.

Deep down, he knew that. His own fears of not being accepted for himself had kept him from seeing Kylie for the woman she was. *What a fool I am.*

"Thanks for the Chinese, Ryan." Kylie interrupted his revelation. She looked at her watch. "The meeting starts in about twenty minutes."

"You feel up to going?"

Kylie shook her head. "I think I'll stay home tonight."

"You want me to stay with you? We can rent a funny movie or just hang out."

"No. You go." She picked up her Bible from the shelf under the coffee table. "I think I'm going to spend some time in this tonight."

Ryan stood and kissed her forehead. "I'll be praying for you."

Kylie opened her Bible. A slip of paper fell onto her lap. "It's the verse from the singles' fellowship." She read it. " 'He who pursues righteousness and love finds life, prosperity and honor,' Proverbs 21:21."

The phone rang, and she laid the paper and the Bible on the coffee table. She answered the call, and a man with the invitation company asked to speak with Robin. "She's not here right now, but I'll tell her you called."

Kylie laid down the phone, then started to clear the table. The proverb swam through her mind. Life, prosperity, and honor—she'd wanted them since she was a small girl.

She wanted a life free of financial worry. Her mother always said she was silly and too sensitive, but Kylie hated feeling bad for asking her parents for money for a movie or for a snack after school. She knew everything she asked for would be a hardship for them. Sure, her sisters and brothers didn't seem to have qualms about asking, but Kylie didn't want to add any strife.

Prosperity. Her parents never had it, but God had given Kylie a smart mind. She was a clear thinker; school came easy to her, especially math. "I know writing isn't my strength." She opened the refrigerator and stuck the leftovers inside. "But despite what Professor Nickels thinks, I won an award in high school for my persuasive letter about the dangers of strip-mining, and I did well in all my college English classes." No, her parents had never prospered, but God had given Kylie the necessary talents to help her family.

Her mother's eyes, gleaming with pride when Amanda announced she was having twins, slipped into Kylie's thoughts. A vision of her daddy hugging Mama and thanking her for supper followed swiftly behind. They'd always said God had blessed them beyond measure. Kylie never quite understood them.

And honor. If she had anything to do with it, Kylie would never have a child of hers receive a free lunch. Her son would never be sponsored for field trips or extracurricular sports. Her daughter would never wear someone else's prom dress. Instead, Kylie would be the one to give those things to someone who needed it. She'd pay back all that she'd received as a child. "Isn't that what God calls us to do? When we've been given, we pull ourselves up, and then give more than we've received."

Something sounded wrong with her words. They felt funny. She couldn't put her finger on it. After throwing the food wrappers in the trash, she scraped the plates and placed them in the dishwasher. She wiped off the counters, then grabbed a bottle of water from the refrigerator and headed back to the couch.

She picked up the slip of paper and read it again. " 'He who pursues righteousness and love finds life, prosperity and honor,' Proverbs 21:21." Flipping to the reference in her Bible, she added, "My reasons for working hard have always been driven by righteousness and love. I don't know why this verse keeps tripping me up."

Kylie devoured the chapter. Each verse, a nugget of wisdom from Solomon, spoke of many things from the wicked to the mocker to the ill-tempered wife. Verse two pricked her heart and she read it again. *All a man's ways seem right to him, but the Lord weighs the heart.*

"My ways seem right to me, Lord." She gazed out her window, past the parking area, past the other homes, and toward the horizon. The land was flat, but she could see the tips of trees in the distance. A clear, blue sky blanketed their tops. "What is the weight of my heart, Lord?"

Her parents, her siblings, they seemed to line up in her soul, displaying their peace in good times and bad times. The Nelsons, gracious and thankful, spilled into her mind. Contentment gleamed from their faces.

Sweet, kind Ryan flooded her thoughts. She had no idea where he got his means, but he always gave of all he had. His heart overflowed with generosity. She relished every moment with him. He never despaired over financial gain, for right or wrong reasons.

It wasn't financial stability they needed. It was God, plain and simple. Their walk with the Lord made them rich, not poor. Proverbs 22:2 screamed at her from the page. *"Rich and poor have this in common: The Lord is the Maker of them all."*

Kylie fell to her knees in front of the couch. "Forgive me, Jesus. My pursuit has been my own. In my pride and self-centeredness, I let the world's standards dictate my worth. I have been a fool."

A tear, warm and refreshing, slipped down her cheek. She clasped her hands and lifted her eyes toward the ceiling. "My life belongs to You. My past. My present. My future. In poverty or wealth or somewhere in between, I don't want to live another moment concerned about the wealth of this world."

Scriptures from Matthew filled her. "God, I don't want to store up treasures from this earth. You are my treasure, Lord. Weigh my heart, and find me full of You."

She stood, walked to her room, and grabbed her cell phone from the shelf. Searching her directory, she found Candy's number then pushed it. Candy's voice sang, "Hello," over the line. Kylie inhaled as peace enveloped her soul. "Candy, I'm going to take that position with the ministry."

sixteen

Ryan couldn't get Kylie off his mind as he stocked cans of green beans and corn on the shelves at God's Pantry. She'd changed over the last few weeks. Eager to raise money for the missions trip, she'd participated in a bake sale and a parents' night out with members of the team. Her eyes danced, and smiles warmed her lips on a regular basis, and Ryan longed to be with her more. He'd been watching for the right time to tell her about his reasons for not working, but he hadn't had a moment alone with her.

Welcoming a couple, Gramps opened the door, and a gust of cool November wind swept through the small building. "Awful cold to not even be Thanksgiving," Gramps's voice boomed.

"Sure is," a man responded.

"Hello. How are you?"

A familiar female voice said, "Did your grandson come today?"

Ryan strolled down the aisle to find Kylie's mom and a man standing beside Gramps. "Mrs. Andrews, it's so good to see you again." Ryan extended his hand. She grabbed him in a hug instead.

"It's good to see you, too. This is my husband, Richard." She patted the man's shoulder.

"You must be Ryan." Mr. Andrews shook his hand, then turned his head to cough. The slump in his shoulders gave away his fatigue and illness. Ryan could tell he'd been a strong man, but black lung was taking its toll on him. He stopped coughing and looked back at Ryan. "Lorma can't seem to stop talking about you."

"How's Kylie?" she asked. "We seem to be playing phone tag."

"She's great. Working hard to raise money for the missions trip and going to school."

"The last I talked to her, she found out she wasn't getting that job she wanted. We've been praying for her." Mrs. Andrews clucked her tongue. "Kylie worries something fierce over having things all laid out nice."

Mr. Andrews cleared his throat. "Life just isn't always like that. Praise the Lord, He's in charge."

"Amen to that." Gramps patted Richard's back.

Mrs. Andrews handed a sack to Ryan. "We came to give back the cans and boxed foods we didn't use."

"You didn't need to do that." Ryan tried to hand it back to her.

She lifted her hand. "No. The good Lord blesses us with what we need each time we need it. Richard's disability checks are coming in now."

"That's right," Mr. Andrews interrupted. He reached into his shirt pocket and pulled out a check. "There's a time to give and a time to receive. We needed to receive from this pantry for a while. Now God's allowing us to give a bit back."

"You're a wonderful couple." Gramps accepted the check.

"I'd like to ask one thing in return." Mrs. Andrews looked up at Ryan. "Can I have another hug?"

Ryan laughed as he leaned down and embraced the older woman. She whispered, "Take care of my Kylie."

"Always." He released her, and she smiled and nodded her head.

Ryan watched as the couple made their way to their car. Though Mrs. Andrews was the driver, her husband opened the door for her and then walked to the passenger side. She leaned over and kissed his cheek before buckling her seat belt and starting the car.

"Kylie has a great family," said Gramps as he sat to write

down the donation in the ledger.

"Yes, she does."

"Did you notice that Richard's coat has seen better days?" A sparkle lit Gramps's eyes.

"You know, Gramps, I hadn't noticed, but now that you mention it, Mrs. Andrews's coat wasn't in too great of shape, either."

"Hmm." Gramps hunched over the desk and calculated some numbers.

Ryan pushed a cart filled with laundry detergents that needed to be placed on the shelf. "We'll just have to take care of that."

❦

"God," Kylie mumbled, "I'm trusting in You." She arranged the Christmas-colored hair bows on the table for the craft bazaar. Having raised only a third of the money she needed for the missions trip, Kylie was depending on a good turnout today to even consider making the missions trip.

"Hey, Ki." Ryan walked toward her, his arms weighed down with wooden poles.

"What are these?" Kylie took a couple from his hands.

"They're Christmas poles to put in your front yard." He grabbed one. "This one's for you."

Kylie looked at the pole painted white. At the top was a piece of red-painted wood that stuck out like a street sign, reading KYLIE'S KOTTAGE. A smiling cardinal sat perched on top, wearing a Santa's hat.

"This is adorable."

"Thanks. Gramps and I love to make them."

"How much are you selling them for?"

Ryan scratched his jaw. "I haven't thought about it."

"Haven't thought about it?" Kylie furrowed her eyebrows. "Aren't you worried at all about raising enough money for the trip?"

"Not really. You see, I need to talk to you—"

"We open the doors in five minutes." Candy scanned the room. "Is everyone ready?"

"Sure are!" a man yelled.

Kylie poked Ryan's arm. "You were saying?"

Ryan furrowed his eyebrows, looked at his poles, and mumbled, "It's never the right time."

"Right time for what?"

"Oh, nothing. I don't worry about the money. God's already provided." Ryan stared into Kylie's eyes as if he were trying to tell her something.

Kylie squelched the urge to rationalize and crunch numbers in her head. She knew God used practical means. She'd also learned He cared more about the heart than the way the money was provided. Her heart had no doubt. For this missions trip, God wanted her to trust Him. She smiled. "You're right."

Kylie placed her signs displaying the cost in front of the different-sized bows. She counted her change drawer one last time.

Customers filtered into the building. A woman with two daughters walked to her table. "These are pretty, Mom." The younger, dark-haired girl touched one of the nicer, silk ribbon bows.

"They are adorable." She picked up several. "I'll take all of these."

Kylie quoted her price, placed the hair bows in a bag, then took the money. "Thank you so much."

The woman moved toward Ryan's side of the table. "This is so cute." She picked up a pole similar to Kylie's except it had four cardinals on top of the sign.

"Look." The older, red-haired girl pointed to the birds. "It's a daddy, a mommy, and two kids. It's just like us."

"Yes, I believe you're right." Ryan picked up the pole. "How 'bout if I do this?"

Kylie watched as Ryan picked up a paintbrush, dipped it in green, then painted a bow on the mother cardinal and the two smaller birds.

"Now, they're girl kids." Ryan laid down the smaller brush and picked up a bigger one. "What's your last name?"

"Sims," the girls answered in unison.

Ryan painted the name on the sign and handed it to the mother. "Be careful. It won't be dry for a while."

"How much does it cost?" The woman reached into her purse.

"Not a thing." He winked at the girls. "Have fun."

Within moments, several people flooded their table, having heard the tall redhead was giving away free decorative poles. Ryan directed them to Kylie's side of the table as he personalized signs for different customers. Two hours before the bazaar ended, Kylie had sold every bow, and Ryan had given away all his signs.

"That was a productive day." Ryan closed his paints and wrapped his brushes.

"For me." Kylie shut and locked her money box. "Did you make anything?"

Ryan shrugged.

"Well?"

"No, but you sold all your bows."

Kylie studied Ryan. Not an ounce of concern for raising enough money etched his face. She now had enough to cover a little more than half the trip's expenses, but as far as she could tell, Ryan hadn't raised a penny.

He leaned closer. "If it makes you feel any better, Gramps and I always make those to give away. We love it."

A smile tugged at her lips. "God always provides for you."

"Every time." Ryan drew closer still until a wisp of his hair caressed her cheek. Her heart sped as goose bumps covered her skin. "Let's grab a burger."

She swallowed, unable to speak. If she tilted her head just slightly she'd be able to kiss him. The idea sent a wave of excitement through her veins. Instead, she nodded.

"Come on." He stood and grabbed her hand. "We're heading out, Candy."

She looked up from her table. "Out of stuff to sell?"

"Yep."

"Okay. See you later."

Kylie slipped into Ryan's car. The urge to kiss him still made her knees weak. She noted the stubble on his jaw and wondered at its roughness. His lips, probably soft, would contrast. . . . She shook her head. *What am I thinking?*

"You want a burger or a sit-down meal?"

"Oh, no." Kylie looked at her watch. "It's Saturday."

"Last time I checked."

"With the bazaar and all, I completely forgot. I'm supposed to try on my gown for Robin's wedding in an hour."

"Not a problem. We'll grab a burger and head over there."

"Thanks, Ryan."

❧

Ryan tried to make himself comfortable in the boutique's stiff chair. The thing was small enough, he felt sure his over-six-foot, two-hundred-plus-pound frame would break it in pieces.

"Honey," the gray-haired woman with a tape measure draped around her neck called into the fitting room. "I'll be right back. I've got another customer who's ready for me to set up her alterations."

Ryan scanned the room. Dresses of every color and style hung from the walls. Several mannequins sported different ones, as well. Headpieces and shoes and other sparkly things sat in nearly every crevice of the shop. The place was completely overwhelming. He couldn't imagine anyone finding what they wanted.

"Where did the seamstress go?"

At the sound of Kylie's voice, Ryan turned toward her and sucked in his breath. The dark red dress, bare of straps, exposed her small neck and the curves of her collarbone. The material flowed down her frame, hugging her perfect shape. It looked soft, and he yearned to touch it. "Wow."

When her cheeks and neck flushed, Ryan knew his mouth gaped open. She was beautiful! Standing, he couldn't stop himself from walking to her. "I thought all eyes were supposed to be on the bride on her wedding day."

The crimson color on her skin deepened as she looked down.

Ryan cupped her chin in his hands. "I know I won't be able to take my eyes off you."

Not able to tear away from her eyes, he watched as her gaze traveled from his jaw to his mouth, up to his eyes, then back to his mouth. She lifted her lips, ever so slightly, and Ryan could take it no more. He lowered his mouth and claimed his first kiss. Her lips, soft and sweet, welcomed his.

Pulling away, Ryan swallowed the desire raging within him. He touched her cheek. "Oh, Ki, you are so beautiful."

"Okay, let's have a look at the dress," the seamstress's voice sounded from across the room. Ryan stepped away as the woman scurried toward them. "Oh, honey." The woman placed her hands on her hips. "That dress fits you like a glove. You're gorgeous."

"I'd say." Ryan sat back into the chair. All the stuff in the shop faded. Everything except Kylie.

seventeen

Kylie crept into her mother's kitchen. Mama, testing the turkey, was bent over with her head practically stuck inside the oven. Her oldest sister, Sabrina, peeled potatoes, her back facing the door. Amanda sat at the table, chopping celery. Kylie wrapped her arms around her younger sister. "Amanda, you are absolutely glowing."

The blond dropped her knife and gasped. "Kylie Andrews, you scared the life out of me." She stood, and Kylie's jaw dropped. Amanda punched her arm. "Hey, I am carrying twins."

"But you're huge!"

Amanda clamped her lips together and crossed her arms in front of her chest. "Mama!"

"Kylie." Her mother hustled over to her. "Women in the family way don't like to be addressed like that." She grinned. "Come here, and give your old mama a hug and a kiss."

"Yeah." Amanda stuck her tongue out, then smiled. "Wait 'til you see Natalie."

Natalie waddled into the kitchen, holding a casserole dish of banana pudding. She brushed a dark wisp of hair away from her cheek. "What about Natalie?"

Kylie reached out both hands and touched each sister's belly. "I don't know who's bigger."

"Har, har, spinster sister. Your day will come—eventually." Natalie smirked.

"Good one." Amanda gave her a high five.

"Mama, Amanda called me a spinster," Kylie squealed.

"Girls, you're acting like toddlers." Mama grabbed a dishrag and wiped her hands. "We've got work to do. Sabrina, Amanda, go back to your potatoes and celery. Kylie, you chop up some onion. Natalie, I want you to whip up those brownies."

Kylie grabbed a knife and a cutting board from the drawer. Grabbing an onion from the sink, she peeled off the outer layer and rinsed it. "Why did I get stuck with the onion?"

"Because Natalie and I will throw up," Amanda answered.

"Did you see Mama's new coat?" Sabrina asked, as she scraped potato shavings into the trash can. "It's the nicest thing I've ever seen."

"Your daddy got one, too." Mama scurried out of the kitchen like a child on Christmas morning. When she returned, she carried in one hand a long, chocolate-colored London Fog trench coat with a thick, plush lining. A full-length, lined, navy coat with a multicolored matching scarf hung from the hanger in her other hand.

"They are beautiful." Kylie fingered the soft material. "Where'd you get them?"

"We don't know. The pastor said someone bought them for us. He couldn't say who."

Bile rose in Kylie's throat. Charity. She hated when people felt sorry for them. If she'd been able to have that job at Miller Enterprises, her parents would have never wanted for anything again.

"I better put these away before we get food on them." Mama walked out of the kitchen.

"We hoped you'd have a guest with you this year," said Natalie.

"Yeah, all this talk about some man. What was his name?" asked Sabrina.

"Ryan," said Mama as she walked back into the kitchen.

Talking about Ryan lifted her spirits some. "I thought about inviting him." Goose bumps covered Kylie's arms when she thought of the last time she'd seen Ryan. At the boutique. She'd never felt so scared and alive all at the same time. Her reaction to his kiss had surprised her.

"Why didn't you?" asked Mama.

"I don't know." Kylie walked to the sink for another onion. "Mama, there's no more in the sink."

"There's some in the drawer of the fridge."

Kylie opened the refrigerator. "Uh-oh, Mama. Someone's been in your deviled eggs."

Mama jumped up and hustled to Kylie. "That daddy of yours. He can't ever wait until suppertime. Richard!"

Dalton ran into the kitchen, his face white as an eggshell. "Mama, come quick!"

"What is it?"

"It's Daddy."

Kylie followed her mother and sisters to the living room. Her daddy sat in his brown chair, gasping for breath. He held his left arm. "Lorma, something doesn't feel right."

"Oh, sweet Jesus, help my Richard. Where are you hurting?"

"My chest. My arm."

"I'll get an aspirin." Sabrina ran into the kitchen while Kylie grabbed the phone and dialed 9-1-1. Mama coaxed the medicine down Daddy's throat. She held his hands and prayed over him.

Please, God. Please don't take Daddy yet. An eternity seemed to pass while they waited for the ambulance. Finally, it arrived and Kylie watched as the paramedics loaded him into the back. Mama jumped in beside Daddy.

Loading into two vans and a car, Kylie, her sisters and brothers, and their families followed behind. The hospital came into view, and Kylie watched as the ambulance pulled into the emergency-room entrance. Her father was unloaded from the back and rushed inside.

Dalton parked his car, and everyone filtered out. Kylie couldn't move. "Go on." Kylie motioned when Dalton extended his hand to her. "I'll come in a second."

She watched as her family disappeared into the hospital. Fear mounted inside her. Tears welled in her eyes. *Not on Thanksgiving, Lord. Please, don't take Daddy yet. We still need him.* She pulled her cell phone from her front jeans pocket and dialed Ryan's number.

"Hello."

"Ryan." Kylie's voice caught in her throat.

"Ki, what's wrong?"

"I—I need you."

"Where are you?"

"At the hospital in Petersburg. My daddy's having a heart attack."

❧

Breathless, Ryan ran into the hospital's emergency-room waiting area and spied Kylie. He rushed to her and wrapped his arms around her. "I got here as quick as I could."

She nestled her face into his embrace and tightened her arms around him. "I know. I need you here so much."

His heart melted. He'd scale a mountain, swim an ocean, fight a lion—anything he needed to do to take care of Kylie. "Have you heard anything yet?"

She pulled away but grabbed his hand. "Not yet."

A large, young man approached and offered his hand. "I'm Dalton. You must be Ryan."

"It's nice to meet you. I wish that it were under different circumstances."

Dalton tried to grin, but his eyes remained weighted and dull. "We're going to keep praying."

Kylie peered up at Ryan. "I won't introduce you now. I'll just point out my brothers and sisters. The boy and the girl at the pop machine are Chloe and Cameron. The pregnant lady on the phone is Natalie. The one on her cell phone is Sabrina. Amanda is the other pregnant one. You just met Dalton. Gideon's the tall, thin one leaning against the wall. The boys are my nephews and the other men are my brothers-in-law—oh, I'll introduce you later."

The doors leading to the back burst open. Mrs. Andrews walked out and clasped her hands. "He's going to be okay."

Ryan rushed over with Kylie and her family as they surrounded her mother. "What's wrong with him, Mama?" one of the siblings asked.

Mrs. Andrews cupped her nearest child's jaw with both hands. "Indigestion." She released her youngest son and wrapped her arms around Amanda. "Your silly, silly daddy ate half a dozen deviled eggs and gave himself a bad case of indigestion."

"Thank You, Lord," whispered Kylie. Ryan squeezed her hand.

"Ryan!" Lorma grabbed him in a hug. "I'm so glad you're here."

Kylie frowned. "You know Ryan?"

"Yes, we met at God's Pantry. He and his grandfather volunteer there."

Ryan felt Kylie's grip loosen. *Don't pull away, Ki.* He tried to squeeze her hand, but she pulled away.

"Why were you at God's Pantry, Mama?"

"We went a few times before your daddy's disability checks started." She looked around at her family. "Who wants to see Daddy first?" Before anyone could respond, Mama grabbed Chloe and Cameron and guided them back through the door.

"You help at God's Pantry, too?"

"Gramps has for years. I've just been helping him the last few times."

"My family paid you a couple visits, and you didn't tell me?"

How could he tell her his mother asked him not to? She hadn't wanted Kylie to worry. He should have never agreed to keep it from Kylie, but he didn't want her to be upset, either. Her self-imposed embarrassment about the times her family lacked financially was ridiculous. He wanted her to get past the money—with him, with her family. He thought she had.

"Someone bought my poverty-stricken parents brand-new coats. Did you know that?"

Ryan swallowed. She couldn't possibly know he bought those coats. He'd sent them through the family's pastor. The man himself didn't even know Ryan's name.

"Is there anything else I can share with you? Any charity *you'd* like to give?"

"What is the matter with you?" Ryan tried to grab her hand. "An hour ago you needed me because you thought your dad was in serious condition; now you're mad because I saw your parents at God's Pantry? I don't care about your family's lack of wealth. I care about you." He touched her cheek. "I love you, Ki."

Contentment glazed her eyes. For a moment. She shook her head. "I'm sorry, Ryan." She moved her face away from his hand. "I shouldn't have called."

eighteen

Kylie hugged her father longer than usual. Willing herself never to forget it, she inhaled his scent, a musky, sweet mixture of aftershave and butterscotch. "Daddy, I—"

"I'm okay, honey." He squeezed her then held her at arm's length. "Just one more month and this family has its first college graduate. I'm proud of you."

She tore her gaze from his. The sincere pride in his eyes made her want to cry—again. "Daddy, I'm going to help. . . ."

He lifted her chin with his thumb. "Now you listen to me. The best help you can give me and your mama is to follow the Lord. He will lead you in the right way."

"I will. God will give me a job where I can make sure you get your medicine and—"

"Kylie." Her father clasped her hands in his. "God has always provided for your mama and me. Always. It's not your job to provide. You, honey, you have to follow God's plan for your life."

"Okay, Daddy." She kissed his cheek and walked to her car. After starting the ignition, she pulled onto the country road leading to the interstate.

It's not okay. God, I want to trust You, but seeing Daddy taken by stretcher into the hospital. . . She shuddered. *There was nothing I could do to help him. Nothing.*

Glancing to her right, Kylie saw the old abandoned church she and her family used to attend. The congregation had long ago outgrown it and built a new one. She drove into the lot and shut off the engine. Envisioning her sisters, baby dolls in tow, standing beneath the large oak tree, she could also see her brother Dalton trying to coerce Gideon into eating a bug.

Smiling, she left the car and walked toward the swing that hung from one of the oak's limbs. Sitting on it, she swung back and forth, allowing the cool November wind to whip through her hair. She looked toward the church's door and remembered Chloe and Cameron toddling around her mama's legs and Daddy shaking hands with the preacher.

Hopping off the swing, she made her way to the back of the property. A small creek was barely recognizable with the grass and weeds grown up all around it. A giggle welled in her throat. "We used to hunt crawdads here."

She looked past the creek at the forever-flowing land before her. In summer, rows of corn would grace it. She remembered a time when Daddy got mad at her, Sabrina, and Natalie because they'd chased Amanda into the rows, then left her there. *We were so ornery.*

Glancing at her watch, she realized it would be dark before she made it back to her apartment. She ambled back to her car and got in. She looked at the church again. "We had a lot of fun."

She pulled back onto the main road. "Even when we didn't have anything."

⁂

"That woman is without a doubt the most infuriating person on the planet." Ryan smacked his keys onto the cabinet.

Gramps sat at the kitchen table, whittling a piece of wood. He didn't even look up. "Ya love her, huh?"

Ryan kicked off his shoes and slid into a chair beside Gramps. Ryan raked his fingers through his hair. "Yes, I love her. I even told her so."

"What did she say?"

" 'I'm sorry. I shouldn't have called.' " Ryan snipped the words in a mocking tone.

"Hmm."

"One moment she's all flustered about me. 'What does Ryan do for money? Is he a thief, a moocher off his grandpa?' The next moment she's all mad because her parents saw us at the pantry when they got food there."

"Hmm."

"I don't know why I even care. How could I fall in love like this again? Vanessa—"

Gramps laid down the piece of wood and his knife. "Kylie is nothing like Vanessa."

"I know." Ryan rested his head against the table. "She's making me crazy. I don't know how I can convince her—"

"How you can convince her?" Gramps huffed and swatted the air. "Seems that's the problem with both of you. It's all about you."

"What do you mean? I'm not doing any—"

Gramps lifted his hand to stop Ryan. "Sometimes God wants us to sit still and listen—to Him. Kylie is so worried about taking care of her parents and making sure she never lives poor again that she can't see what God is giving her."

"I agree. But you said both of us. I'm trusting God."

"Are you, son? Are you really? You're so worried about her being like Vanessa that you won't give Kylie a chance. Worse yet, you won't give God a chance to show you that Kylie is not after your money."

"But—"

"I'm too old for all this." Gramps pushed himself up out of his chair. "Why don't you sit still a second and see what God tells you?"

Ryan watched as Gramps made his way up the stairs. *I have been trusting You, God. I've tried to tell her several times.*

The Holy Spirit spoke to his heart. *"Then why didn't you?"*

He slipped his shoes back on and walked out onto the porch. Lowering into a rocking chair, he watched the sun sink into the horizon. Yellows and deep oranges blanketed the earth. Ryan couldn't help but wonder at God's creativity and brilliance.

"You painted this picture, Lord. The heavens and the earth proclaim Your majesty. Why am I afraid to tell Kylie about the wealth You've given me?"

He walked back into the house and grabbed his keys from the counter. He made his way back to the car. "Because I haven't completely trusted You. Forgive me, Lord."

Pulling out of his driveway, he drummed the steering wheel. "Now what should I say, God? 'Um, Kylie, I know you think I'm living off Gramps, but really I'm loaded.' " He shook his head.

"What about, 'Kylie, I'm sorry I never told you, but I have the means to provide for you for the rest of your life.' " He groaned. "God, I feel like a total idiot."

An idea sprang to mind. *Thank You, Lord.* He raced to the bank and withdrew the money he needed from the ATM. A smile lifted his lips as he made his way to Candy's house. Glancing at the clock on the dash, he sighed. "I don't think it's too late."

He pulled into Candy's driveway and hopped out. His heart sped up when he rang the doorbell. Footsteps sounded inside, and Ryan feared his heart would pound through his chest at any moment.

With Suzanna planted on her hip, Candy opened the door and grinned. "Hey, Ryan. Come on in."

Ryan stepped inside. "Thanks. I won't stay long."

"What can I do for you?"

"I want to pay for the rest of Kylie's trip. How much does she need?"

Candy's eyes bulged as a smile formed on her lips. "That's wonderful. What a load off her shoulders! Here, take Suzanna; I'll go find out."

Before Ryan could say otherwise, Candy placed the wiggling

baby in his arms. Suzanna grabbed his hair with one hand. She laughed when she yanked a few strands from his head. "Aren't you a little spitfire?" Ryan pried her fist open and wiped his hair away from her slobbery hand.

"This is what she owes." Candy returned, took the baby, and handed him a slip of paper. Ryan handed her the money. Candy's eyebrows lifted as she looked up at him. "She's going to want to know who paid for it."

"Yep, she will. Don't tell her it's me; just say this exactly: 'The person who paid for the rest of your trip wants you to know God always provides, Ki.'"

" 'God always provides'?"

"No." Ryan shook his head. " 'God always provides, Ki.'"

Candy shrugged. "Okay. You got it."

Ryan waved before Candy shut the door behind him. He jingled his keys as he headed toward his car. The sun had set. God graced the sky with the moon and a sprinkling of stars. "I pray Kylie gets it, too."

nineteen

Kylie trudged up the sidewalk toward her apartment. She unlocked the door and walked inside. Exhausted from her trip, she plopped her suitcase and purse on a chair. After kicking off her shoes, she trailed into the kitchen for a pop. She glanced at the answering machine on the counter. "Eight messages! Has Robin even checked this thing?"

Probably not, she realized. Robin spent precious little time at the apartment as she planned her wedding and spent time with Tyler and Bransom. *Three days, and I won't have a roommate.*

The finality of it hit hard. It had taken time, but Kylie had come to believe her friend would be content as a wife and mother. Still, the change stung. Maybe it wasn't the change, but the glimmer in Robin's eye, the lilt in her voice, the bounce in her step.

Brushing the thoughts aside, Kylie pushed the MESSAGE button on the answering machine.

"Message one," the English-accented recorded voice announced.

A *click* sounded. Someone hung up on the machine. Kylie pushed DELETE, then listened as the next two messages were the same. "Why do people wait until they hear the entire 'Leave a message' spiel and then hang up?"

"Message four." Kylie always smiled at the computerized pronunciation of the number.

"Hey, Robin," Tyler's voice boomed through the room. "I'm running a little late."

Kylie deleted the days-old message.

"Message five."

"Hi, Robin," her own voice, as well as muffled activity from her parents' home, spilled from the machine. "I wanted to wish you a happy Thanksgiving."

She pushed the DELETE button. She'd called before her father's rush to the hospital. *I miss them so much already.*

"Message six."

"Hi, Kylie." Candy's voice held a hint of laughter. "I have the best news for you. Someone has paid for the remainder of your trip."

"What?" Kylie leaned closer to hear better as excitement welled within her.

"The person didn't want me to come out and tell you who he was, but to say, and I quote, 'God always provides, Ki.'"

"God always provides, Ki?" She furrowed her brows. "The only person who would say that, who calls me Ki is—"

"Message seven."

"Hello, Kylie, this is Brad Dickson at Miller Enterprises."

Kylie sucked in her breath at the sound of his voice. *What could he possibly want?*

"It seems we have another opening in our office. Mr. Miller would like to offer you the position, but he needs you to begin as soon as you graduate, mid-December. If not, we'll need to get someone else in here. We're in a bit of a crunch, and there're a few other qualified candidates to choose from. Call as soon as you get this message."

I can have the job again?

"Message eight."

"Hi, Robin. This is the florist. . ."

Stumbling from the kitchen, Kylie's messages churned in her stomach. She plopped on the couch, laid her head back, and stared at the ceiling. "I can go on the trip. I can have the job."

She blinked. "But not both."

Candy's message from Kylie's benefactor swam through her mind. "God always provides, Ki."

"No one but Ryan calls me Ki." She sat up and stared at the wall. "But how could he possibly afford to pay the rest of my way? He hasn't even earned money for his."

She stood and ambled to the bathroom. Resting her hands on the vanity, she stared at her reflection. "I can have a job at Miller's again. I'll make enough money there to provide well for my family and me."

But the job is demanding, and I won't be able to go on the missions trip.

Her heart sank. She thought of the hours Mr. Miller expected of his employees. Well above the forty-hour workweek. Financially, she could help her mama and daddy, but she'd rarely have time to see them. She stared at the mirror. "I miss them so much, and I just saw them earlier today."

The goals she'd set for herself were finally coming to fruition. She could easily tell the ministry leaders she had reconsidered and decided to work at Miller Enterprises. This was her chance, but she didn't feel happy. Not even excited. Nothing. . .but heaviness.

She grabbed a towel and washcloth from the linen closet and turned on the shower. "I just need to rest a minute. Let all this sink in."

After feeling to make sure the water was hot, she pulled the ponytail from her hair. *"God always provides, Ki."* The words slipped into her mind. She closed her eyes. "Oh, sweet Jesus, guide me."

❧

Ryan strode into the jewelry shop. Clear glass counters adorned each wall. Deep red and green fabric hung like fancy curtains above the counters. A covered display of possible Christmas gifts "for that special someone" sat on a circular, center table.

"May I help you, sir?" A short, balding man approached.

"Yes. I've come to pick up my order. For Ryan Watkins."

The man nodded. "Very good. I'll be right back."

Ryan walked to a counter, pulled his wallet from his back pocket, and dug through it for the receipt. The gift cost too much for any dispute over whether it had been paid for.

"Here we go." The man rested the box on the counter.

Ryan handed the man the receipt, then opened the side and pulled out the silver plate with Tyler's and Robin's names as well as their wedding date engraved into it. Joshua's proclamation, "As for me and my household, we will serve the Lord," scrolled across the center in calligraphy.

To him, this was a silly, frivolous gift. But Gramps insisted. Every wedding he always insisted.

"It's a tradition," he'd say. "When your grandma and I married, her favorite gift was her silver plate. For every wedding we attended, she bought the same for the newlyweds."

Ryan slid it back into the box. "It looks nice. Thank you."

"Is there anything else I can help you with?"

"I don't believe so."

Ryan turned to leave, when he saw a young woman trying on a ring. She extended her hand and gazed at it. The man beside her leaned down and whispered in her ear. She stood on tiptoes and kissed his cheek.

A sudden longing for Kylie stirred him. No more games. No more waiting. He knew he loved her. Knew he wanted to spend the rest of his life with her. *God, I've already given the whole money thing over to You.*

The time had come.

He glanced back at the clerk. "I may look around a bit."

"Very good. Let me know if I can help you with anything."

Ryan looked in the case that held the engagement rings. So many round diamonds in varying sizes shone back at him. Some rested in yellow gold settings. Some in white, and still others in platinum. He moved farther down and noted the different settings. The rings seemed much the same as the round ones, only now the stone had a marquise shape.

Moving still farther down, he came to a section of multiple-stoned rings. Many were large and gaudy. One in particular with three huge stones caught his eye. He huffed. "Vanessa would have wanted that one."

Ryan shook his head. Kylie was nothing like Vanessa. *Thank You, Lord.* Another ring caught his eye. The white gold band had a center, circular diamond, resting in a square setting. It wasn't overly large, but it was a nice size. Smaller diamonds adorned both sides, with even smaller stones outside of them. The ring had an antique appearance. Somehow it made him feel the commitment, the longevity of the promise it held.

Ryan motioned to the man for assistance. After showing the one he wanted to view, the man placed it in Ryan's hand. He pushed it onto his pinky. *It's perfect.* "I'll take it."

❧

Kylie glanced to the left, then right in the church's foyer. Empty. She adjusted the top of the strapless bridesmaid dress, then quietly peeked around the corner of one door.

Family and friends filled the small church to capacity. Deep red rosebuds and baby's breath arrangements adorned the side of every third pew. Just beyond the altar rested an elaborate wedding arch dressed in crimson velvet and white satin. Full-bloom roses wrapped around the unity candle.

Tyler and the groomsmen had already taken their positions in the front. They looked handsome in their matching black tuxedos and red cummerbunds. Only Tyler wore black with a white vest.

She scanned the crowd. If Kylie didn't hurry and get back to the wedding party, Robin's mom would faint for sure. Kylie had never seen a mother so frazzled. *Where is Ryan?*

"Kylie."

Kylie jumped, then placed her hand on her chest to calm her heart. "Ryan, you scared the life out of me. I was just looking for you."

"You were?" His eyebrows rose in interest.

Heat raced up her neck and cheeks. Seeing him now, she knew she missed him more than she'd realized. His eyes, honest and compassionate, bore at her soul. The playful, stray curls at the base of his neck begged to be touched. "Yes, well. . ."

"You're absolutely gorgeous."

"Thank you, I—"

He bent down toward her. She lifted her chin, willing his kiss. Instead, his breath brushed her ear. "I better find a seat. I'll talk to you at the reception."

"Okay." She blinked. What just happened? *I just felt an attraction I've never experienced in my life.* Opening her heart and mind to God over the last few days, she'd felt a peace she hadn't known in years. She'd been trying to get hold of Ryan to ask him about the missions trip money and tell him about her job decision. He hadn't been home. But the electricity she'd just experienced at his closeness had wiped all that from her mind.

At the quiet chattering behind her, she hurried back to Robin and the bridesmaids. They hustled into their line as the music began. When it was Kylie's turn, she began her slow ascent to the altar. Peering to her left, she found Ryan. He watched her with such longing her knees grew weak. Tearing her gaze from him, she focused on putting one foot in front of the other.

What is happening, Lord? This feels like more than attraction. She took her place as maid of honor. *I've said time and again I'm falling for him, but I could always rationalize myself through.*

She sneaked a quick peek at him. He smiled, and she knew he hadn't stopped watching her. *I don't want to rationalize, Lord, and it feels right.*

Gripping the bouquet tighter, she listened as Tyler and Robin recited their vows. She wanted more than the perfect husband, the perfect kids, the perfect dog, the perfect white picket fence. The perfect job. She needed more. She needed love. *"The pursuit of righteousness and love."*

Looking at Ryan again, she smiled when their gazes met. Yes, love.

❧

Ryan touched Kylie's hand. "Have I told you how beautiful you look?"

A blush crept up her cheek, adding to her innocent beauty. "A few times." She shrugged, then nudged his shoulder. "But then a girl never tires of hearing it."

Ryan laughed. "I've been trying to reach you."

"I've tried calling you, too."

"I think we're playing phone tag."

She nodded.

"How is your dad?"

"He's doing great. I—I wanted to apologize for how I treated you at the hospital. I was under a lot of stress then. I've been doing a lot of praying this week. Someone told me that God always provides. . . ." She stopped and winked at him.

She got it. She knows it was me who paid for her trip. This is my chance, Lord. You've shown me the time.

"Kylie, I—"

"Kylie." Tyler's best man grabbed her arm. "I've been looking everywhere for you. I want to pray a blessing for Tyler and Robin before they cut the cake."

"Okay." Kylie stood and smiled at Ryan. "I'll be back."

Ryan's heart sank as she walked away. He yearned to finish their conversation, but as the evening progressed, her duties continually called her away.

After several hours passed, Ryan noticed her step slowed and her shoulders slumped ever so slightly. Once the newlyweds were nestled into their car and headed to the airport, Ryan touched Kylie's arm. "You want me to take you home?"

"I'm going to help clean up. Plus, I drove." She stepped closer to him. "But I still want to talk."

Every manly urge within him wanted to grab her into his arms, to caress the exhaustion away from her face. He swallowed and shoved his fists into his pockets. "How 'bout I take you to dinner and then the Festival of Lights tomorrow night?"

"Oh, I love the lights. That sounds wonderful."

He kissed her forehead. "I can't wait."

twenty

Kylie plopped onto the wooden chair. "It's early in the morning, the weekend, and I'm at school." She slipped the book bag from her shoulder and dropped it to the floor beside the computer station. Clicking the computer mouse, she waited for the machine to wake up. Glancing around the university library, she sighed. "But this may be my last time in here."

The bittersweet reality pricked at her heart. For four years her focus had been on the pursuit of this prize—her degree. Not just a degree but one with the highest of honors. Summa cum laude. She figured the better the grade point average, the more likely she'd be to land a good, solid accounting position.

UNIVERSITY OF EVANSVILLE scrolled across the screen. She clicked the school's icon, moved through the system, then typed in her screen name and password. Once the computer recognized her, she scrolled down the options until she came to GRADES.

She took a deep breath. There was no way she could get an A in Nickels's class this semester. She may not get a B. Failing her first test and doing only fairly well on the project, her grade depended on the final exam. Which had been excruciatingly difficult. If she received a C, she wouldn't receive highest honors.

Tapping the bottom of the mouse, she couldn't seem to make herself click the screen. A bit of trepidation sailed through her veins, but not what she would have expected. Just a few short months ago, during the summer, she'd been stressed to the max about a possible B in Nickels's class. Now the possibility of a C didn't *truly* faze her.

So much had happened this last semester. She thought her daddy might die of a heart attack. Miller Enterprises offered a job, took it back, then offered one again. Robin got married. Ryan—

The thought of Ryan brought a smile to her lips. *Kind. Considerate. Gentle. Handsome. Godly.* He was everything she'd ever wanted in a man. *But without a steady job.* She chuckled and shook her head. Of all the requirements for a mate she'd ever had, her top two had been that he love the Lord and that he have a good, steady income. Ryan met only one.

Somehow, I'm all right with that.

Studying the options before her on the computer screen, she shrugged. "Might as well get it over with."

She clicked for her grades. The class courses popped on the screen. Within a second the grade followed. She bit her lip and grinned. "Three As and one C."

After closing her account and then the screen, she picked up her bag and slung it over her shoulder. She had several books she needed to return in hopes of getting some kind of refund. Glancing one last time at the library, she grinned as peace flooded her soul. "I'm not summa cum laude, and it's okay."

❧

Ryan unbuckled the oversize black belt, then folded off the Santa suit and extra padding. The air had been nippy for the town's annual Christmas in Santa Claus Parade, but sweat still beaded on his forehead due to the mass of padding. He didn't mind. Seeing the children of the community's faces light up when his sleigh approached them had been priceless. As he passed, he tried to make sure each one received a candy cane from Santa.

He peeled off the white beard, mustache, and eyebrows. Rubbing the now-tender places, he hoped his face wouldn't be red for his date with Kylie.

"Tonight's the big night, huh?" Gramps, adorned in a bright green shirt and candy cane suspenders, strolled into Ryan's bedroom. Large, red pointy shoes with bells stitched at the tips covered the man's feet. A matching hat sat on his head.

Ryan shook his head and chuckled.

"Oh, so it's okay for you to dress up like Santa Claus, but I can't be an elf."

"Are you kidding? You look great. Heading to Santa's Lodge for the concerts?"

"Yep, then St. Nick's Restaurant for dinner. Wouldn't miss the gingerbread decorating for the world."

"Hmm. I'm not sure if it's the decorating or seeing Elma that you like so much."

"Tosh, son." Gramps swatted the air. "That woman drives me crazy. Did you see her hair at church on Sunday? It's back to blue! Blue, pink, blue, pink. You'd think the woman would make up her mind."

Ryan laughed out loud.

Gramps moved closer to him. "I think you're avoiding my question."

Ryan cleared his throat and glanced at his closet. "What question?"

"I asked if tonight was the night."

"The night for the Festival of Lights? Yep. It sure is."

Gramps shook his finger. "Don't play coy with me. If you don't want to say, then don't say."

Ryan smiled. "I'm just teasing. Yes. Tonight's the night."

A sparkle lit Gramps's eyes. "I'll pray for you."

"That would be great."

≈

Kylie gazed at her reflection in the full-length mirror. The shimmering blue dress flared at the skirt as she twirled around. In truth, it was a bit fancy for a simple dinner and tour of the lights date. Flutters filled Kylie's stomach as she prayed Ryan had something more in mind.

"I can't believe I want to marry the man." She touched her cheeks when they began to blaze with the desire that filled her whole being. She closed her eyes. "Please, Lord, let him ask me tonight."

Bending over, she picked up her high-heeled black shoes. She sat on the bed and put them on. Standing again, she twirled once more in the mirror. Her feminine instinct yearned for Ryan to find her breathtaking.

The doorbell rang, and Kylie glanced at the alarm clock on her nightstand. "He's a full half hour early." Kylie walked to the front door and peered through the peephole. "Brad?"

Turning away, she leaned against the door, contemplating if she should pretend not to be home. Her heart pricked. "I know, God; that would be wrong." Taking a deep breath, Kylie unlocked and opened the door. She plastered a smile to her face. "Hello, Brad."

Brad whistled and eyed her up and down, again making her feel cheap. "Where are you going, babe?"

She inhaled a deep breath and bit back a retort regarding his lack of manners. "Did you need something, Brad?"

He leaned against the door frame. "You want to invite me in?"

"I don't have much time." She planted her feet firmly in the doorway.

He leaned closer to her, and Kylie didn't budge. He lifted his hands in the air. "Okay, okay. I quit. I just came to see if you were going to take the job."

Kylie frowned and folded her arms in front of her chest. "I've already talked to Mr. Miller."

"Oh." Brad snapped his fingers. "He may have mentioned that."

"What did you come for, Brad?"

He shrugged and slinked into one of her chairs on the porch. "I don't know. Thought you might want to go out sometime." He peered up at her, and for once Kylie saw a hint of sincerity in his eyes. "I haven't met anyone like you, Kylie. Most girls fall all over me."

Kylie bit the inside of her lip. Even his attempt at honesty was laced with his inflated ego. Still, it was the first attempt at truthfulness she'd seen from him since her first interview when Mr. Miller had been present. "I can't go out with you, Brad."

"It's that Ryan, isn't it?"

Warmth flooded her heart at the mention of his name. "Yes."

Brad stood and started down the sidewalk. "Well, it was nice meeting you, Kylie."

A twinge of guilt filled her. "Brad." She walked toward him. "I would love it if you would come to my church sometime. We have a really great singles' group. You'd probably enjoy yourself."

Brad half grinned. "I might do that."

28

Ryan gazed at Kylie from across the booth in the restaurant. She was a vision of beauty with her hair held away from her face with a clip. Small wisps distracted him as they caressed her neck with each move of her head. Her bright blue dress enhanced her eyes, which shone against her creamy skin. "You're stunning, Ki."

Her cheeks reddened as a smile of pleasure bowed her lips. "Thank you."

"I think you'd make a garbage sack beautiful."

"Ryan." She smacked his hand. "You're silly."

He inwardly growled at her playfulness. She had no idea how much he yearned to take her in his arms and kiss her sweet lips.

She grabbed his hand. "I have some news for you."

He relished the softness of her skin. "I have something

I want to tell you, too."

She removed her hand, and he missed her warmth. "Okay. You first."

Ryan shook his head. "No. Go ahead."

"Okay. First, I got a C in Nickels's class. No highest honors for me."

He grimaced, knowing how much her grades meant to her. "I'm sorry."

"It's okay." She shrugged. "It's really okay." Her eyes glistened with the smile that graced her mouth. "I got another job offer with Miller Enterprises, but it starts in December."

"That's. . .great." Ryan tried not to frown as his heart fell into his stomach. She wouldn't be going on the missions trip, and that job would be so time-consuming.

"I turned it down."

"You what?"

She giggled. "Yep. I turned it down. This person, who remains nameless, paid for my missions trip. He said that God always provides. Well, I've been praying and searching, and I know God wants me to go on that trip. More importantly, He wants me to trust Him with my life. I was offered the position with the missions ministry, and I'm taking it."

"Oh, Kylie."

"I know you paid my way, Ryan. I've wanted to thank you—to tell you that I have deep feelings for you. I've—I've struggled with a lot of things, but I—I. . ."

Ryan's heart swelled. Excitement coursed through him. "Kylie." He placed his finger across her lips. "I have to tell you something first."

He took her hand in his, caressing her palm with his thumb. "About eight years ago, I fell in love with a woman. I thought she was everything I was looking for. Until she found out about. . ."

Ryan took a deep breath. This wasn't the way he wanted to

tell her. Ryan cleared his throat. "Let me start over. There's a reason I don't work a nine-to-five job. When I was in high school, I developed a machine to make logging easier. I sold my blueprints to a company in Alaska. I made a good amount of money from the sale, and then Gramps invested big chunks of it into different stocks and bonds."

He watched as her eyes widened. "I don't understand."

"Vanessa, the woman I mentioned before, she loved my wealth, not me. I swore I'd never tell anyone about the money again. If God ever placed a woman in my life, she'd have to love me for me."

"You thought I'd love you for your money?"

"When I first saw you, you were talking to Robin about *yahoo* men, and you were so focused on getting through school to get a good-paying job."

He watched as her shoulders slumped a bit as she let out a breath. Her gaze lowered to the table, and she moved her hand from his. "I see."

"No, you don't. I was wrong. I wasn't putting my trust in the Lord or you. I was too worried about what Vanessa had done. Ki." He grabbed her hand again. "I love you."

She gazed up at him. Uncertainty filled her eyes. In a rush, Ryan reached into his pocket and pulled out the ring box. He knelt beside her and opened the box. "Please, Ki. You're the perfect woman for me. The one God intended. I love you. Marry me."

Tears filled her eyes as she slowly shook her head. "I don't think I can."

twenty-one

Kylie bit into her hamburger. The stale bun and overcooked meat stuck to the roof of her mouth. She sighed as yet another mall-going, happy couple walked past her.

"What is the matter with you? You've acted all day like you lost your best friend." Amanda swiped a fry from Kylie's tray. "Our annual Christmas shopping trip is supposed to be fun."

Kylie halfheartedly gazed at her more-pregnant-than-ever little sister. Amanda's hair looked fuller and healthier as it framed her sickeningly glowing face. She rested a protective hand on her belly as she drowned the fry in ketchup then shoved it into her mouth. A drop fell on the top arch of her stomach. Amanda giggled as she licked her napkin and wiped it off.

Amanda's happiness made Kylie's stomach whirl. Kylie wrinkled her nose. "Just grouchy, I guess."

Amanda eyed her. "I'd say you're more than grouchy. Remember, big sis, we shared a room far too long for you to play games with me. What gives?"

Kylie twirled her straw in her now-runny chocolate shake. "Ryan asked me to marry him."

Amanda's mouth popped open and her eyes glistened with excitement. "That's great! Please, Kylie." She placed her hand on Kylie's. "Please tell me that you have realized that you love this man. It's so obvious to the rest of us."

"I do love him." Kylie tried to sip the milk shake, but it pooled in the back of her throat, making her feel nauseous. Her gaze found a teenage couple walking by hand in hand.

"But—"

"But I told him no."

"What?" Amanda smacked her napkin onto the table. "Kylie Andrews, why?"

"He's been lying to me all this time."

"Lying to you? About what?"

"He's rich, Amanda." Kylie pushed the tray away from her. "I don't know how rich, but enough that the man doesn't even have to work."

"Okay." Amanda furrowed her eyebrows. "So Ryan is rich. He didn't come right out and tell you, but now he wants to marry you. I'm not following the problem here."

"Some girl he used to love wanted him for his money or something like that, so he didn't tell me because he didn't want me to want him for his money; he wanted me to want him for himself." She flailed her arms and shook her head. "Oh, he just didn't trust me to tell me, okay?"

"Kylie."

"He knew how much I wanted to help take care of Mama and Daddy. He knew I was trying so hard to get a good job. He knew how afraid I was of ending up married to a coal. . . miner." Kylie lowered her gaze. "I'm sorry, Amanda."

"Kylie." Amanda placed her hand on Kylie's arm. "I love my coal-mining husband. So, so much. And he loves me. And he loves the Lord. I wouldn't trade my life for all the financial stability in the world." Amanda let go of Kylie's arm, then folded her hands on the table. "I'm sorry for you, Kylie."

Kylie frowned at her sister.

Amanda closed her eyes. "God's given you a wonderful man with the financial stability you've always dreamed about." Amanda opened her eyes and let out a deep breath. "And you still don't see it."

&

Ryan grabbed a bag of potato chips from the pantry then opened the refrigerator and took out a can of pop. After snatching the remote control from the coffee table, he fell into the oversize recliner. Restless, he flipped through stations. Nothing interested him. He stopped on a station showing a commercial and dropped the remote on the end table.

"Still sulking?" Gramps's voice sounded from the couch where he lay facing the cushions, arms around a pillow.

"I thought you were taking a nap."

Gramps turned around and pushed the pillow behind his head. "I reckon a man can't sleep with the racket you're making."

"Sorry." Ryan shoved a potato chip in his mouth, then washed it down with a swig of pop. The commercial ended.

"*It's a Wonderful Life* is on." Gramps sat up. "I love this movie."

Ryan groaned. Great. *It's a Wonderful Life. Oh, yes. Mine is absolutely terrific.* He crunched another chip. *Like I haven't seen this a million times anyway.*

"You're becoming unbearable to live with." Gramps reached over and grabbed a handful of chips from the bag.

"I'm not even saying anything."

"It's what you're not saying."

"What?"

"You asked Kylie to marry you a week ago. Now you're not saying much of anything." Gramps looked at him. "Tell me what happened."

Ryan shrugged and watched the screen as Jimmy Stewart threatened to throw himself off the bridge. At this moment, Ryan understood Jimmy's need, his feelings of complete failure. "She said no."

"Just like that." Gramps folded his arms in front of his chest. "No."

"Just like that."

"Did she say why?"

"She didn't want me when I didn't have money. Now she doesn't want me because I do. Now, in my thinking, that means she flat out just doesn't want me." Ryan leaned back in his chair and looked at the ceiling. "I thought she was about to tell me she loved me, but—what does it matter now?"

"You're probably right." Gramps stretched his arms over his head. "Think I'm going to head over to St. Nick's for a cup of coffee. You wanna come?" He swatted the air. "Nah. You oughta stay here and watch some television." He stood and patted Ryan's shoulder. "You haven't done much of that lately."

"Are you making fun of me?"

"I'd never do that." Gramps grabbed his coat off the rack and slid into it. "I'll see you in a bit."

Ryan watched as Gramps stepped out and shut the door. He offered no "I hate that for you, son." No "I'm so sorry." Ryan frowned as he looked back at the screen. Jimmy Stewart raked his hand through his hair in grievous frustration. Without the money, his place would close and so would his life. *Money. It's always about money, and I'm sick of it.*

❧

"Just a minute!" Kylie called through the apartment when the doorbell rang. She grabbed an oven mitt then pulled the Christmas cookies from the oven. "I'm coming." After taking the mitt off her hand, she brushed a few wayward wisps of hair behind her ear.

She peeked through the peephole. "Gramps?" After opening the door, Kylie motioned for him to come inside. "I haven't seen you in a while. How are you?"

"Good."

She pointed toward the couch, then sat in a chair. Wringing her hands, her heart sped in nervous anticipation. She had no idea what Ryan had said and if Gramps was mad or hurt or what. "Have a seat. How's—how's Ryan?"

"Miserable." Gramps didn't move. Instead, he crossed his arms in front of his chest.

Kylie looked at her hands. She picked at a chip in one of her fingernails as a mixture of relief and sadness filled her spirit. "Oh."

"Is that all you have to say? 'Oh'?"

She gazed up at the older man. He'd cared about her from the moment she met him. He was the perfect gramps, a little rough around the edges, a bit of a spitfire, too, but with a heart filled with love, generosity, and loyalty. Her grandparents died when she was young, and she'd enjoyed Ryan's grandfather as if he were her own. "I don't know what else to say."

"All right. Let's figure this out, because I'm thinkin' your feelings for Ryan run deeper than you want to admit."

"Well. . ."

He scratched his gray-stubbled jaw with his fingers and paced the floor. "When you met Ryan, you thought he was a bit of a yahoo—"

Kylie's mouth dropped open. "How would you know—?"

He raised his hand to stop her. "Ryan mentioned it."

Her cheeks blazed hot at the memory, at the thought of what he must have felt when he heard her talking. People never ceased to surprise her. As soon as she was sure she had someone pegged, she'd learn there was more to them than she realized. "I judged him wrong."

Gramps clucked his tongue. "Which is why God tells us not to judge people."

Kylie nodded, feeling the swell of emotion in her throat. "You're right. God and I have talked a lot about that over the last few days."

Gramps smiled as he paced away from her. "You thought Ryan was a poor guy, one who didn't even work a full-time job. Can't say I blame you for not wanting to jump into a relationship with him. He was a bit silly not to trust God with you from the very beginning."

Kylie smiled. At least Gramps understood why she'd been blown away.

Gramps sat on the couch across from her. "But now you know the truth. You know he has the means to provide for you. You know he didn't tell you because of what happened in his past. I believe you know he loves you with all his heart, and you love him. It's nothing more than pride and arrogance that keeps you from him."

"You're right."

"Huh?"

Kylie giggled. "You're right. It's been pride. I've had my mind on one goal for so long. The one I know God did give me. I just wasn't prepared for *how* God planned to bless me with it. I thought He would give me a job in a prestigious company with a business-oriented husband all wrapped up in a neat package." She stood, walked to the table, and picked up the handmade Christmas card she'd made for Ryan. "But God had a different plan. A better one. Ryan."

Gramps leaned back in his seat. He tapped the arm of the couch as he bit his lip, then chuckled. "You were heading over to the house to talk to Ryan, weren't you?"

Kylie nodded. "Just as soon as I got up the courage."

"I'd be happy to go with you."

"I think I'd appreciate that."

Gramps stood and walked toward her. He wrapped his arms around her, and Kylie savored his hug of understanding and acceptance. "That boy's been unbearable. I'd like to get you on over there just as quick as I can."

Kylie laughed and squeezed him tight one more time. "Let's go."

"You can ride over there with me, then Ryan'll have to bring you home." A twinkle lit Gramps's eye, and he winked at her.

Nervousness filled Kylie's gut as she slipped her shoes on and grabbed her coat, and they headed toward the front door. Ryan may be miserable to live with, but that didn't mean he was ready to welcome Kylie into his heart with open arms. She opened the front door and ran into a mass of man. "Ryan?"

❧

"Kylie." Ryan lowered his hand from the doorbell. Deciding he couldn't take it anymore, he'd turned off *It's a Wonderful Life* and headed to her apartment to talk with her one more time. He looked past Kylie. "Gramps? What are you doing here?"

Gramps buttoned the top of his coat and moved past Kylie and out the door. "I reckon it's time for me to go on home."

"Gramps." Ryan glared at his grandfather. "What were you doing?"

"Go on in there." Gramps practically pushed him into Kylie. "Talk to the woman." He hustled down the sidewalk. He mumbled, "Didn't I say I was too old for all this? Young people these days. . ."

Ryan turned back toward Kylie. Her eyes sparkled, but he couldn't decide if that was from happiness at seeing him or nervousness that he was there. "Can I come in?"

"Oh, yeah, yeah." She stepped backward and tried to pull off her coat all in one motion, then tripped on the rug. Her arms flailed in an attempt to catch herself.

Ryan tried to grab her arm to stop her fall. Instead, he gripped the coat sleeve and her arm slipped through it. She landed with a *thud* on the floor. Ryan stepped forward to help her. "Oh, Ki, are you—"

His foot caught on the rug and he launched forward, landing on his hands and knees beside her. "Ouch." He turned over and sat beside her, rubbing his knees. "You didn't have to drag me down here. I've already fallen for you."

"Ryan, are you okay?" She took his hands in hers and rubbed the red spots on his palms.

Ryan clasped both her hands in his. "I came over here to tell you I love you. I'm not letting you get away from me. I'm going to sit right here in your living room until we talk everything out and I've convinced you that we belong together."

She lowered her gaze and slipped her hands from his. "Do you mind if we sit somewhere besides here?" She pointed to the open front door. "It's kind of cold outside."

He hopped to his feet, shut the door, then reached down and helped her up. He held her close and peered into her eyes for the briefest of moments. "I love you, Ki."

Letting go of her hand, he walked farther into the apartment. "It's like this. I was convinced you had feelings for Brad. I was afraid you were like Vanessa. Yes, my heart told me that wasn't true, but I was so focused on the past that I wasn't listening to God clearly."

He walked toward her again. "I should have told you from the beginning. Of course, you were afraid I couldn't provide for a family. I was—"

"Ryan." She grabbed his hand in hers, caressing his palm with her thumb. Fire raced through him, blazing a trail of desire to convince her to be his wife. After all, God had brought them together.

"You have to understand—"

"Ryan." She lifted up on tiptoes and brushed her lips against his. She lowered to her height and gazed into his eyes. "You gotta hush a minute."

Ryan swallowed. The sweet softness of her lips took him by surprise. He was hushed. Stunned to utter silence better described it. "Kylie." He leaned toward her to claim another kiss, one that he could enjoy without surprise.

She pushed a paper into his hand. "I was coming to your house to give you this."

Ryan looked at the homemade card that had a photo of himself dressed as Santa in the Christmas parade. In it, he held a small candy cane in his hand, offering it to a child. Opening the card, he saw pictures cut from magazines. First of a chocolate ice-cream cone, then a clown suit. Next was a cutout of canned foods and cereal boxes, then a winter coat. She'd taken a picture of her Christmas pole and glued it on there as well. Around the edges of the card were crayon-drawn, stick-figure people holding hands.

Kylie cleared her throat. "I'm not overly crafty. Look at the back. That's what I was getting at."

The back contained no pictures, just Kylie's handwriting. She expressed her journey over the last several months with him—how she'd found him to be the most generous, loving person she'd ever known. She shared how God had showed her to pursue Him, not specific goals. Ryan's heart warmed as she wrote how she'd fallen in love with him, the man, before learning he could provide for her.

"I still love the man." Kylie quoted the last sentence of her letter. Her face flushed and she lowered her gaze. "It's kind of a silly thing, a full-grown woman making a man a homemade card, but I—"

Ryan closed the card, laid it on the table, then wrapped his arms around her. "It's the best present I've ever received. Only one could be better."

He reached into his jeans pocket and pulled out the ring box. After popping it open, he lowered to his knee and took her hand in his. "I love you. Marry me."

Her eyes lit with merriment as she knelt beside him. She wrapped her arms around his neck and kissed him on the lips. "Absolutely," she replied after she pulled away.

Ryan huffed as he placed the ring on her finger. "You've kissed me twice today. I have yet to kiss you."

"You take too long." She claimed his lips again.

"Never again." He stood and helped her up. Wrapping his arms around her, he lifted her up and kissed her with the fullness of his love. He lowered her to her feet, then brushed her hair away from her face. He caressed her soft cheek with his thumb. "I'm holding on to you for the rest of my life."

twenty-two

May

Ryan felt the buttons on his tuxedo jacket to be sure he hadn't missed one. He raked his fingers through his hair.

"Nervous?" Gramps, his best man, poked Ryan's side.

"A little."

"No cold feet." Dalton leaned over past Gramps. He nodded toward his other brothers, Gideon and Cameron, as well as Tyler. "We'll take you out if you even consider leaving our big sis at the altar."

Tyler laughed at Ryan. "I believe they could take you, friend."

Dalton winked and showed his newly covered ring finger. "Nah, seriously. It's a piece of cake."

Ryan watched as Dalton waved at his bride, Tanya. She blushed as she fidgeted with one of Amanda's twin sons. The other started to fuss, and Amanda's husband picked him up. The only baby girl in the family, Natalie's new daughter, sat contently on her daddy's lap.

A laugh formed in Ryan's gut as he thought of the ever-growing family he was marrying into. He and Gramps had lived so long with only each other. Both of them relished becoming part of Kylie's family. "Don't worry, Dalton. I'm not going anywhere."

"We're about to begin," the minister whispered to them.

Ryan straightened his shoulders, watching as one of their ushers escorted Kylie's tearful mother to her place in the audience. She smiled at Ryan as she scanned the row of groomsmen—his grandfather, all three of her sons, and Tyler. Ryan knew Mrs. Andrews thanked God for each of her children and their choices in spouses. Ryan felt blessed and honored that she and Mr. Andrews approved of him.

The music began and Chloe, Kylie's youngest sister, made her way to the front. Next came her oldest sister, Sabrina. "Mommy!" her barely two-year-old son yelled from his father's lap. Everyone laughed as her husband whispered in the small boy's ear. The child squirmed and waved until Sabrina finally motioned for him to stand beside her at the front. He toddled forward, grabbed her leg, then popped his thumb into his mouth.

"What a cutie," Gramps whispered.

Ryan nodded. Anticipation welled in him as another sister, Natalie, walked toward the altar. Next came Robin, then Amanda. Kylie had deemed them both her matrons of honor. Ryan squeezed his fists. With all her last-minute errands and hair appointments and whatever else she did, he'd only seen Kylie at the rehearsal and the dinner that followed. They'd hardly spoken two words together that someone else hadn't instructed them to say. And it was killing him.

Kylie and her father stepped into the aisle. Ryan sucked in his breath.

"She's a beauty, even with her face covered," Gramps whispered.

Ryan couldn't respond. He nodded and asked God to help him remember every detail of his bride as she and her father walked toward him.

"Who gives this woman to this man?" the minister's voice boomed through the church.

"Her mother and I do." Kylie's father lifted the veil over her face and kissed her cheek. Her gaze found Ryan's. Ready to claim his bride, Ryan puffed out his chest, longing to shout to the world that beautiful Kylie Andrews had chosen him.

He took her hand in his and led her to the altar where they made their vows. The promise, the covenant, the commitment weighed his heart with a heaviness of bliss and contentment. In sickness, in health, in good, in bad, whatever life held, he would honor his vows to the woman God had given him.

When the minister instructed, he kissed her as his wife, then took her hand in his and faced their family and friends.

"I now present to you," the minister addressed the audience, "Mr. and Mrs. Ryan Watkins."

Ryan scooped her into his arms and started down the aisle.

"You're supposed to carry me over the threshold of our home," she whispered into his ear, trying to control her giggles.

"I told you I'd never take too long again." He kissed her cheek.

She nestled into his chest. "You did say never again."

"Never again."

❧

Kylie glanced down at her watch, afraid they would miss their plane to Belize. The missions trip in January had been an experience she'd never forget. She'd fallen in love with the people in the community. They were planning another trip in two months, in July. Today, they'd go as honeymooners and visit their friends there. "Are you sure you have to have whatever it is you forgot?"

Ryan smiled and tapped the steering wheel. "I thought I could wait, but I can't."

Kylie scrunched up her nose. "What?"

He turned the corner and started toward his house. "Close your eyes, Ki."

"What is going on?" She clamped her lips in a straight line, trying not to smile at him.

His lips bowed up. He bit the bottom and frowned, in a pitiful attempt not to grin. "Just close them."

"Okay." Kylie shut her eyes, then popped one open.

"Kylie Watkins!"

She squished them shut. "I like the sound of that."

"Me, too." He stopped the car and hopped out. Everything in Kylie wanted to open her eyes and look around, but she didn't want to spoil his surprise. Her door opened, and Ryan's hand took hers.

"Can I open them?"

"Nope." He gently pushed her head down then out of the car. "Be careful." He wrapped his arm around her as he guided her steps. Her heels crunched against the gravel driveway. "Okay, open your eyes."

Kylie opened them to find Gramps standing in front of her, holding a small, golden retriever puppy. "Oh." Kylie took him in her arms. "He's so cute."

"Didn't you say you wanted a godly husband, two kids"—he gathered her in his arms and whispered in her ear—"which I'm willing to work on. . ."

Her neck and cheeks warmed under his sincere, longing gaze.

He continued, "A dog and—"

She smiled and lifted her eyebrows to tease him. "I think you're forgetting something."

"No, Ki, I'm not." He turned her around, and she gasped. A white picket fence scaled the entire front of his home. One of his handmade poles stood next to the porch with their names written on the sign and two cardinal birds perched on top.

"A white picket fence." Kylie held the puppy closer to her chest, then gazed up at the man of her dreams. The man who listened to all the things she longed for. The man who wanted her to have them all.

"Oh, Ryan." She put the puppy down in the yard then touched Ryan's cheek with her hand. "There isn't a more wonderful man for me in all the world."

She stood on tiptoes and kissed his lips. With all her heart, she had pursued what she thought God had called her to—a family, a job, stability. When she finally gave over control to her heavenly Father, He lavished her with everything she had ever pursued. She gazed at her new husband. Only more. Right down to the white picket fence.

A Letter To Our Readers

Dear Reader:

In order that we might better contribute to your reading enjoyment, we would appreciate your taking a few minutes to respond to the following questions. We welcome your comments and read each form and letter we receive. When completed, please return to the following:

Fiction Editor
Heartsong Presents
PO Box 719
Uhrichsville, Ohio 44683

1. Did you enjoy reading *Picket Fence Pursuit* by Jennifer Johnson?
   ❏ Very much! I would like to see more books by this author!
   ❏ Moderately. I would have enjoyed it more if

   _____

   _____

   _____

2. Are you a member of **Heartsong Presents**? ❏ Yes ❏ No
   If no, where did you purchase this book? _____

   _____

3. How would you rate, on a scale from 1 (poor) to 5 (superior), the cover design? _____

4. On a scale from 1 (poor) to 10 (superior), please rate the following elements.

   ____ Heroine   ____ Plot
   ____ Hero   ____ Inspirational theme
   ____ Setting   ____ Secondary characters

5. These characters were special because? _____

_____

_____

6. How has this book inspired your life? _____

_____

_____

7. What settings would you like to see covered in future
   Heartsong Presents books? _____

_____

_____

8. What are some inspirational themes you would like to see
   treated in future books? _____

_____

_____

9. Would you be interested in reading other **Heartsong
   Presents** titles? ❏ Yes ❏ No

10. Please check your age range:
    ❏ Under 18   ❏ 18-24
    ❏ 25-34   ❏ 35-45
    ❏ 46-55   ❏ Over 55

Name _____

Occupation _____

Address _____

City, State, Zip _____

NEW HAMPSHIRE
Weddings

3 stories in 1

Three New Hampshire women are living their lives on their own terms, each struggling with the need for change and fulfillment.

Titles by author Rachel Hauck include: *Lambert's Pride*, *Lambert's Code*, and *Lambert's Peace*.

Contemporary, paperback, 384 pages, 5³/₁₆" x 8"

Heart♥ng

Presents

Great Inspirational Romance at a Great Price!

Heartsong Presents books are inspirational romances in contemporary and historical settings, designed to give you an enjoyable, spirit-lifting reading experience. You can choose wonderfully written titles from some of today's best authors like Andrea Boeshaar, Wanda E. Brunstetter, Yvonne Lehman, Joyce Livingston, and many others.

When ordering quantities less than twelve, above titles are $2.97 each.
Not all titles may be available at time of order.

SEND TO: **Heartsong Presents** Readers' Service
                P.O. Box 721, Uhrichsville, Ohio 44683

Please send me the items checked above. I am enclosing $ _____
(please add $3.00 to cover postage per order. OH add 7% tax. NJ
add 6%). Send check or money order, no cash or C.O.D.s, please.

      To place a credit card order, call 1-740-922-7280.

NAME _____

ADDRESS _____

CITY/STATE _____ ZIP _____

                                                  HP 4-07